For Jim,
A new friend in
Baltimore —
Hope this book is
a hit with you

Warmly
Mel Glenn

Squeeze Play

Also by Mel Glenn

One Order to Go
Play-by-Play

Class Dismissed! *High School Poems*
Class Dismissed II *More High School Poems*
Back to Class

Squeeze Play

A Baseball Story
BY MEL GLENN

Clarion Books • New York

Clarion Books
a Houghton Mifflin Company imprint
52 Vanderbilt Avenue, New York, NY 10017
Text copyright © 1989 by Mel Glenn

Library of Congress Cataloging-in-Publication Data
Glenn, Mel.
Squeeze Play : a baseball story / Mel Glenn.
p. cm.
Summary: With the support of gentle Mr. Janowicz, a Holocaust
survivor, Jeremy speaks out against his bullying sixth grade teacher
and his mandatory after-school baseball games.
ISBN 0-89919-859-7 : $12.95
[1. Baseball--Fiction. 2. Schools--Fiction. 3. Jews--Fiction.]
I. Title.
PZ7.G485Sq 1989
[Fic]--dc19   88-39847
                                                              CIP
                                                               AC
P 10 9 8 7 6 5 4 3 2 1

For Jonathan and Andrew

Contents

1
The First Swing

"Let's go bother your sister," Lloyd says as he bounces a tennis ball against the side of my house. The day feels hot and humid, like I'm walking around in a bucket of water.

"What for?" I say, looking up from my *MAD* magazine.

"I don't know. Nothin' else to do. Isn't she supposed to be in camp?"

"Who?"

"Your sister, brain. Who do you think I mean? Haven't seen her much lately."

"She's working," I say, trying to read and talk at the same time.

"Where?" he says insistently, not missing even one catch. Lloyd seems to be always bouncing, catching, or throwing things. Lately he's been a pain about my sister, always wanting to know what she's like, who her favorite rock groups are, who she's seeing, stuff like that. It's pretty annoying.

"At the card store in the mall," I answer while turning a page.

"The one with the old man?"

"Yeah, that one."

"He's so strange," Lloyd says, finally putting the ball in his pocket. "I know. I've been to the store lots of times. Nobody can understand him. He's got a weird accent or something. Your sister like him?"

"How should I know? Go ask her," I say. "I never speak to Lynne if I can help it."

"Why not, Jer? Your sister's so cool," Lloyd says.

"Get off it, Lloyd," I say. "She's not cool; she's just my sister."

"Tell you what I wish," he says. "I wish I was older and she was younger and we'd meet somewhere in the middle. Ever notice what beautiful hair she has?"

"Lloyd, this conversation is getting sickening. Knock it off. If you like my sister so much, go up and tell her. Go inside the house and tell her. She's probably still on the phone. She was this morning."

Surprisingly, I see Lloyd blush. I can't believe he really likes my sister that much. Unreal.

After a few seconds of silence, Lloyd takes the ball out of his pocket, tosses it into my lap, and changes the subject. "So what do you want to do now?" he says irritably. "We can't just sit around all day. We only have a week before jail starts."

"I don't know," I answer. "It's too hot to do anything. You really think sixth grade will be tough? I heard that the new teacher, Shore, is tough. He's in the army, I heard."

"How can he be in the army and teach school at the same time, jerk?"

"Then maybe he was in the army reserves or something," I say.

Lloyd thinks for a second and then says, "Well, he's gotta be better than what we had last year in fifth. Mrs. Kovin was such a ditz."

"It's gonna be funny having a man teacher," I say. "I wish we could have Mrs. Bedford again."

"Our fourth-grade teacher? Are you for real? She'd treat us like babies. We're in the sixth grade now—almost junior high. But sixth grade ain't here yet. So stop wasting time. What do you want to do?"

"Read," I say.

"We got one week left and you want to spend it reading? Save it for school, Jer. Get a life, man. We could kick around a soccer ball for old times' sake."

"I don't feel like it."

"You don't want to recapture those glorious days of yesteryear?" he says. I know what's coming. Lloyd's play-by-play.

"You don't want to relive those exciting moments when the fourth-grade Sneaker team totally demolished the dreaded Dragon team with a marvelous display of passing, shooting, and scoring, mostly by me?" he says.

"I said I don't feel like playing soccer," I answer, but I'm cracking up on Lloyd's dramatic delivery.

"So what do you want to do?" he says, returning to his regular voice.

"I told you—read. You can go speak to my sister, if that turns you on." That gets him quiet for a second.

"I got a better idea," he says after a few seconds. "Let's go down to McClaren and check out what's doin' there. Maybe some of the guys'll be there. You could use the practice—in any sport."

I stare at him.

"Just kidding, Jer. Can't you take a joke?"

Just before we get ready to go to the park, Lloyd says, "I got it. We're gonna play baseball against the handball wall in the park. We haven't done that all summer. What do you say? Isn't that a great idea? You have a bat in your garage, and we got the ball right here."

"I think the idea stinks," I say. "You know I don't like baseball all that much. It's boring."

Lloyd goes crazy when I say stuff like that about baseball. It's his favorite sport. He has promised me a season's pass to whatever major league team has the good sense to draft him.

"Come on, Jer. Just pitch a few in to me. I need the practice. How can I make the majors if I don't practice?"

Like he really needs the practice. Lloyd, if you haven't guessed by now, is a natural athlete. He eats, drinks, and lives sports. There are all these banners, pennants, and trophies in his room. His closet looks like a pro's locker in any one of three sports. There is only one kid in our class better than him, and that's Billy Cisco. Lloyd's better than Josie, but not by too much. Josie is the best girl athlete in our class. She's better than most of the boys, including me. I don't mind, though; she's not stuck up about it.

"OK, OK," I say, "but don't expect me to hit the strike zone. I can't throw all that accurately."

"Just hit the wall, Jeremy, that's all I ask for. Just hit the wall."

"Cute," I say as we walk over to the park.

When we get to McClaren, Lloyd tosses me the tennis ball he had been bouncing all the way to the park. "Hold it a sec, Jer," he says as he heads for the water fountain near the handball court. "I wanna get a drink."

I look around the park. Sun slants through the trees.

Most people are lazing about, moving slowly, if at all, because of the still strong afternoon sun. "What are you, a camel?" I say to Lloyd as he continues drinking.

"Now I'm ready to play," Lloyd says finally as he wipes his mouth with his sleeve. "You ready to get creamed?"

"I thought you said this was just practice," I say.

"Serious practice," Lloyd says, squinting across the green field that is adjacent to the handball court. "Say, isn't that—what's his name—the old man from the card store?"

"Where?"

"There—over by the benches," he points.

I look to where he's pointing. "I think so," I say. "Wonder what he's doing here. Shouldn't he be in his store?"

"How should I know? Maybe he felt like getting out. It's a free park, you know. Maybe he's walking his dog."

"I don't see any dog. I wonder if I should go over and say hello," I say.

"What for? He doesn't know you."

"He knows Lynne."

"So what? Let's play ball already. Any longer and it's gonna be a night game. You can say hello another time."

Lloyd jogs over to the chalked outline of a box drawn on the handball wall. The box represents the strike zone.

He starts his play-by-play. His insurance, he calls it. If his pro career doesn't work out or if he gets hurt, he's gonna be a network commentator.

He takes a few practice swings and announces: "OK, folks, it's a beautiful day for a ball game, perfect baseball weather, temperature in the seventies and just a few clouds in the sky."

"Are you the weatherman or the first batter?" I say as I swing my arms to loosen up.

"I gotta tell you, folks, the pitcher looks kind of nervous," Lloyd continues. "He's making comments to the batter. The pitcher has just been called up from Triple A, and he might just be feeling overwhelmed in his first major league start. He hasn't faced this kind of talent before. The pitcher also *looks* funny—big nose, weird eyes."

"Cut it out, Lloyd," I yell from the chalked pitcher's mound some forty feet away. I get ready to throw the first pitch.

"OK, he's an average-looking doofy guy," Lloyd teases.

The rules for this game are simple: three swings and you're out; a foul ball counts as a swing; a ground ball past the pitcher is a single, over his head a double, the back fence a triple, and over the fence a home run. I've never hit a home run, but Lloyd has done it dozens of times.

I peer in at the strike zone. Like I really know what I'm doing. Right. I wind up and let fly with a pitch that sails in back of Lloyd's head.

"Well, the pitcher looks mighty sharp today," Lloyd says sarcastically, returning to his play-by-play. "A few more like that and it will be an early trip to the showers for this young right-hander."

I laugh off his comment and stare again at the rectangle. My second pitch comes in low and away.

"That's ball two, sports fans!" he yells out. "This pitcher can't find the plate with binoculars. Come on, just get the ball in, nice and easy. No big deal, a baby could do it."

Stung, I zip the next pitch in tight under his chin and he jackknifes away.

"Oh, the old brushback pitch. A little intimidation here, folks, but this leadoff batter ain't gonna be intimidated. Here comes the next pitch and it's high and wide. The batter trots down to first. Here comes the pitching coach out to settle his young starter."

Lloyd strolls over to me and says, "Do you think I'm standin' up there for my health? Give me somethin' to swing at."

"I'm trying," I say. "Do you want me to pitch underhanded?"

"No, I don't want you to pitch underhanded," he mimics me. "Just get the ball over." He walks back to the wall. "OK, man on first, nobody out. Second man up." (Lloyd swings.) "And there is a line shot over the pitcher's head straight out into center."

"Are you aiming for me or what?" I say, alarmed.

"Men on second and third," he says. "Still nobody out and the number three hitter steps in. He's batting a healthy .306 and is looking to add to his seven-game hitting streak."

The first pitch (I get off a lucky one) is in there for a strike.

I lob in the second pitch. This completely fools Lloyd as he swings so hard that he twists himself into a pretzel.

He rights himself and says, "Two strikes in a row. The pitcher seems to be finding the range now. The batter steps up." (Lloyd swings.) "He lashes the 0-2 pitch up against the fence for a two-run triple. The good guys lead the bad guys 2-0 and there is still nobody out."

Lloyd catches his breath, taps the bat on the concrete, and announces, "The cleanup batter is up next. He's having a banner year, second in the league in RBIs and currently in first place in the balloting for the all-star team. The big third baseman awaits the delivery. The runner dances off third." (Lloyd swings.) "A line drive straight back at the pitch. . . ."

The ball hits me squarely in the face. I don't even have time to bring my hand up. A circle of pain ripples behind my eye as I feel myself falling. I'm lying on the ground for I don't know how long. Then I try to get up on one knee, but I fall back down. My eye hurts, it hurts.

"Stay where you are," I hear an older man say. "Sonny boy, go call 911, quickly, hear me? Run. I wait with your friend."

I feel the man's hand behind my head. "Sssh, *tatelah*, it will be soon good. The doctor will come. Just rest and don't move, not even one muscle."

"Oh, my God, your eye's bleeding." I hear Lloyd say as he runs off. It's the last thing I remember before I pass out.

2

The New Manager

"There is absolutely no way I'm walking out of this house and going to school with this ridiculous patch over my eye. I look like a pirate. They're all gonna make fun of me," I say to my mother at breakfast on the first day of school.

"No, they won't. They might stare for a few seconds and then make you walk the plank," my mother grins.

"Very funny," I say.

"C'mon, Jeremy, stop feeling so sorry for yourself," she says, stirring her coffee.

"Feeling sorry? I get hit in the face, my eye looks like a balloon, I feel miserable, and on top of all that I have to wear this stupid patch. Do you want me to totally die of embarrassment?"

"It could have been a lot worse," my mom says

between sips. "A lot worse. You know that, don't you? If Mr. Janowicz hadn't got you to the hospital, hadn't kept you quiet, hadn't contacted us, I don't know what might have happened. I thank God the man was in the park at that time."

I stare into my Rice Krispies and don't say anything.

"Dr. Meyers promised there would be no permanent injury," my mother says. "The ball cut the lid of your eye. That's why there was so much blood. You're a very lucky boy."

"Why do I have to wear this patch, though?" I say sullenly.

"Dr. Meyers said you had a slight corneal abrasion and the eye needs time to heal."

"Dr. Meyers doesn't have to go to school with this. It's ugly, it's gross, and I hate it."

"Here, I'll do something about that," she says, and before I can protest she takes a pair of old sunglasses from a kitchen drawer and plops them on my nose.

"Mom!" I scream. "I can't wear this. I look like a gangster."

"C'mon, Jeremy, you look like a movie star now," my mom says, pushing away from the table. "Better get a move on. Here's a note for your teacher telling why you have to wear a patch. Let me add on about the sunglasses. I doubt you'll need to explain, but take the note anyway. Good luck on your first day, honey. I know everything is going to be just fine."

It's not that my mother is unsympathetic; she just isn't mushy about stuff. She was very calm at the hospital, constantly reassuring me that I would be all right. Lloyd said that had it been his mother, they would have been peeling her off the walls.

Lloyd rode in the ambulance with me and Mr. Janowicz. At first the paramedics wouldn't let Lloyd in the ambulance. But when he got all excited and yelled, "That's my best friend, I ain't leavin' him!" the paramedics were too busy with me to argue.

I take my book bag and walk on over to the bus stop. On the way there I try to think about who will be on the bus and if they will make fun of me. No doubt the whole world knows about my accident by now. Lloyd probably called up everybody to tell them the gruesome details. Billy and Jason? No problem. Peggy? If she makes a crack about my patch, I'll get her about her braces. Josie's cool. She's one of the guys anyway.

Loretta?

Thank God, she won't be on the bus. Of all the girls in the class, she's the one who'd tease me the most, I'd bet.

Last year she was such a pain, always playing up to the teacher. "Yes, Mrs. Kovin, I would be extremely pleased to be your monitor." "Yes, I'd be happy to take that note to Principal Donovan for you. No trouble at all." Yuck! Sometimes she acted so stuck up, like Lucy in the Charlie Brown cartoon. You know

13

how some people are born with a silver spoon in their mouth? Well, Loretta was born with a service for six.

Lloyd told me that she may not even be in our class this year. He had heard she was going to transfer to Penwell Prep, a very fancy and very famous private school that's a few miles away. The school is so exclusive, I hear it serves three-course meals for lunch.

So after thinking about all this, who do you suppose I see at the bus stop? Loretta, naturally.

"What happened to you?" I say before she can say anything about my eye. "I thought you were going to Penwell this year."

"Well, that didn't work out," she says to me more nicely than I expected. "I got accepted and all that, but my father wasn't sure Penwell was the place for me. He said it would accentuate my sense of superiority. I said to him I have no sense of superiority. I'm just better than anyone else."

"Right, Loretta," I say. "Sure you are."

"Jeremy, that was a joke. Only kidding. I'm trying to develop my sense of humor. It's one of my goals for this year. How am I doing?"

"Too early to tell," I say with a slight smile. "Do you know any jokes?"

"Do I?" Loretta says happily. "Did you hear this one? What do an old car and a baby have in common?"

"Beats me," I say.

"Neither one goes anywhere without a rattle," she says triumphantly. "What do you hear about Shore?"

"I hear that he's mean."

"That's what I hear, too, an ex-officer or something. Maybe he was a Green Beret. You want to hear some good gossip about Shore? Sure you do. My father told me that before he came to our school, he used to teach at Penwell. Can you beat that? Then he got dumped."

"How come?" I ask.

"How should I know? I don't know everything. Just nearly everything. Actually, my father heard that he blew up at the headmaster once too often. So my father's not too thrilled about Shore being my teacher now." She brushes the hair out of her eyes. "Can I ask you something, Jeremy? Why are you wearing sunglasses? A new image?"

"I got hit by a pitch," I explain. It feels good to say that. Manly.

"Does it hurt?" she asks. I am surprised by her concern. It's something new for her, and I like it. "Only when I take the glass eye out," I tell her.

"Jeremy!" she yells. "That's so gross. That's the grossest—"

The rest of her words are drowned out by the roar of our bus, which comes just then.

I see Jason, Billy, and, of course, Lloyd on the bus. I swing into the seat next to Lloyd as Loretta walks past me to a group of girls in the back. Nobody but Cattucci says anything about my eye. He good-naturedly offers me a dog from his parents' pet store. "With a little training he'd be the perfect seeing eye dog," Cat says.

"It's only one eye. Maybe half a dog will do," I shoot back.

We all start talking about Mr. Shore.

"I hear he's very mean," Jason says.

"How mean is he?" we all say together.

Jason thinks quickly. "He's so mean that if you do something wrong, he puts you in a corner and fingerprints you."

"Lame," we all say in chorus.

Billy Cisco says, "You guys are looking at this all wrong. If you walk in there with a bad attitude, looking for trouble, you're gonna find it. I don't think he's gonna be so terrible. He'll give us the usual if-we-all-work-together-this-will-be-a-fine-yearkindof speech. He'll come in with a smile, and we'll all have a good day, you'll see."

For the first time that I can remember, Billy, our class leader, the best athlete, the person everybody respects, is dead wrong.

When we get to our classroom on the second floor, a tall, elegantly dressed man stands in the doorway. He wears a sharp-looking gray suit with a red striped tie. His hair is cut short, crew-cut style, and he has a straight nose and a small mouth. There is no smile on his face, just a piece of paper in his hands, which directs us to an assigned seat in the classroom.

As I squeeze by him he says to me suddenly, "Mr. Martin." I jump and turn around. How come he knows my name already? "Mr. Martin, is there a reason for this unusual disguise of yours?" he says in a low but menacing voice. I am too scared to answer. Everybody is looking at me. I hang my head. "I didn't think so," he says. "Please remove the sunglasses, which are hardly regulation." It is not a request, but a command.

I fumble in my pocket for my mother's note. He reads it quickly and says, "Find your seat, please."

When we are settled into our assigned seats—I'm sitting next to Peggy, who seems to have fewer rubber bands on her braces this year—Mr. Shore closes the door. He stands in front of the room straight and tall. There is not a sound from anyone, just the gentle whir of the air conditioner.

"Good morning," he says without any kind of smile at all. "This is class 6-231. My name is Mr. Mark Shore, not Store or Shaw, but Shore. Please enunciate it clearly. You may call me Mr. Shore or sir."

(How about Supreme Allied Commander, I think to myself.)

"This year I will be your teacher, your mentor, your advisor, your instructor," he continues.

17

(Drill instructor, I say to myself.) I sneak a look over to Lloyd, who gives me a quick shrug of his shoulders, as if to say he doesn't know what to make of this guy either.

"Up to now," Mr. Shore continues, "the world, your teachers, your parents have insisted on treating you like babies. That may have been all right up to now, but starting today it's no longer all right, no longer acceptable. The world is a responsible place, and it is *my* responsibility to make sure you fit in."

(Fit into what, I think.)

"I daresay some of you may have heard of me," he says after a short pause. "I have taught in some of the finest schools in the state, not to mention some prominent local institutions of learning."

I sneak a quick look over at Loretta. We both mouth the words *Penwell Prep*.

"I am an excellent teacher, as you will soon discover. Some of you may balk at my high standards, but I am sure you will come to realize there is virtue in hard work and discipline. The world is highly competitive, and there is simply no room, even in the sixth grade, for people who don't toe the mark."

He takes a breath and then says, "The homework for tomorrow is on the board. Please copy it now."

(Homework on the first day? Give me a break.)

I turn to Lloyd, who gives me a this-guy-is-crazy look.

18

"You should know something about me, I think," he says. "Unclassified personal data, if you will. I'm thirty-nine years old, am in excellent physical health, and love to travel. At the moment I am not married. You should know that I graduated from high school and spent the next several years in the army," he continues. "It was there I found structure and discipline I needed and now wish to pass on to you. The army taught me how to manage my time, my life, and my priorities. I had wanted to make the army my career, but an injury forced me out of active duty.

"Why am I a teacher?, you may ask. I realized after I left active service and decided to go to college on the GI bill that the time to make any meaningful change in a person's life is not during high school or right afterward. By that time the pattern of learning, and indeed life, is set. No, the time to mold young minds is right now.

"The army taught me another thing—baseball." Lloyd looks up. "That great American game. More about that later, but now let's proceed toward our objectives for the day."

("Objectives for the day?" Why doesn't this guy use normal words?)

"At the top of my agenda is my list of rules and regulations for the year, a contract if you like, that will precisely designate and outline what I require from you. Read it carefully and sign it below, attesting to the

19

fact that you have understood its contents. I will collect your signed contracts in ten minutes. Will the first person in each squad, I mean each row, give out these papers and we will proceed according to plan."

At the moment Peggy turns to me and says, "Jeremy, we don't have to sign anything, do we? Can he really make us do that?"

"Ms. Rigby!"

Peggy freezes in midsentence.

"Ms. Rigby," Mr. Shore says more softly, but still firmly. "Maybe I didn't make myself clear. There are two ways in which this class can be conducted—my way and the wrong way. Be so good as to turn around now."

Peggy quickly whips around, locks herself in a rigid position, her hands folded on the desk. I bury my eyes into the paper just handed me and read his contract.

For a brief second I wonder what Mr. Shore would do if I didn't sign his paper. I sign the contract.

Mr. Shore collects the papers and goes on. "This morning we will have a few inventory tests in reading and mathematics so that I may properly place you in appropriate platoons commensurate with your abilities."

("Platoons"? Are we being drafted? And what does he mean by "commensurate"? Why can't he talk in regular English?)

20

At recess the reaction to Mr. Shore is sharply divided. We all agree that we never had a teacher like him. He's certainly not like Mrs. Bedford, who was more like somebody's grandmother, or Mrs. Kovin, who dressed up as a witch for Halloween. Mr. Shore reminds me of a general in charge of a very small country where all the people have to be loyal subjects.

And what about his rules and regulations? They're more like orders from the general to his troops.

I wonder if we have to salute him as well as the flag in the morning.

"Can we order pizza for supper?" I ask my mom when I walk in the door after school.

"School was that bad?" she responds.

My mom knows. Some people drown their sorrows in drink. With me it's pizza. If I feel a little depressed, I get a plain pie. The more depressed I feel, the more toppings I order. The local pizza place even has something called the "Kitchen Sink," which I reserve for disasters like floods, tornadoes, and bad report cards.

"It wasn't that bad, but the new teacher is so strict. He wants us to be mature and responsible."

"That's horrible," my mother says jokingly. "How's the eye?"

"Fine. OK. Listen. You gotta hear about this guy."

"I called Dr. Meyers. He said you have to wear the patch for only a couple more days. Isn't that great news?"

"Ma, you're not listening. He doesn't act like a regular teacher, more like a drill sergeant."

"That may not be so awful. A little discipline might be good for you."

"He gave us homework the first day."

"I like the man," my mother says, smiling. "Give it some time, Jeremy. You'll survive the sixth grade, I'm sure of it."

"Where's the princess?" I ask.

"Working at the card store. Till seven, I believe."

"You mean I have to wait for supper till then?"

"You go do your homework. Afterward I'll order the pizza. What kind do you want? And after supper you can go down to the card store and personally thank Mr. Janowicz."

"Do I have to?"

"Don't you think it would be a nice thing to do?"

"I guess so. Yeah, sure."

"What's the pizza number?"

I tell her. Important numbers like that you memorize. "Did you hear from Dad yet?" I ask.

"No, he's flying to San Francisco today from Kansas City. I'll call him later at the hotel."

"Why'd he go, anyway? He never goes anywhere. He just sits in front of the TV."

"Jeremy, you know the reason as well as I do. The bank sent him. He's training other loan officers."

"You have to teach someone how to give away money? Hey, give me that job. One dollar for me, one dollar for you. I could live with it."

I go upstairs to do my homework. It doesn't take all that long. I make an extra effort to write neatly. No sense in getting on Mr. Shore's bad side. After my homework I find an old magazine and leaf through it.

In a while I hear my mother say, "Jeremy, I think I hear the bell. Go get the pizza. There's money on the shelf."

Just as I'm wolfing down my third slice, the phone rings. "Get it!" my mother shouts from the living room. "Maybe it's your father calling from San Francisco."

It's not my father, but Lloyd. I can hardly understand what he's saying. I tell him to slow down.

"Jeremy, you gotta come with me!" he screams through the wire. "It's the chance of a lifetime to meet him. You'll never get another chance like this in your whole entire life."

"Who? Where?" I say, totally confused.

"At the bookstore in the mall, the Book Shelf. You know where it is, don't you? There's a rumor he's there right now, this very instant. Jason just called me."

"Who?"

"Lou Stryker, the Lion."

"Who's that?"

"Tell me you don't know. Right. What planet have you been living on? He's the most famous National League ballplayer there is. And he's there right now. In person."

"Whoop-de-do," I say. "Baseball is not exactly my favorite sport these days, Lloyd. Why don't you go with Jason?"

"He can't go. He's gotta do something for his mom, and my mom said I couldn't go alone."

"Why don't you try one of the other guys?"

"I did. No one can go. You're the only one left. Jeremy, you gotta do me this favor, you just gotta. It's my one big chance to meet him. I have to see the Lion."

"But you're not even sure he's there."

"I don't care. If he's there and I don't go, I'll never forgive myself. Jeremy, please!"

"OK, OK, I'll go ask my mom."

"I think it's a good idea," my mom says when I tell her. "This way you can go afterward to the card store and thank Mr. Janowicz and then have Lynne drive you and Lloyd home." I tell Lloyd and he hangs up, saying he'll be right over.

When I get off the phone, my mother puts the back of her hand against her forehead, pretends to faint, and says sarcastically, "Lou Stryker, my hero."

"Mom, you know who he is?" I say looking at her in amazement. My mother generally hates sports.

"Sure, I know. Didn't he just sign a contract for two million dollars? I remember reading about it on the editorial page. *I'd* learn baseball for that kind of money. Is he worth it?"

"Lloyd certainly thinks so."

"And he's at the bookstore now?"

"Yep, that's what Lloyd says."

"Well, you better hurry. A man making that kind of money is not going to sit around waiting for you two guys."

3

The Old Veteran

"Where is he?" Lloyd says frantically as he looks all around the bookstore.

I don't see anyone who looks close to a ballplayer, just a lot of people with shopping bags. "I think you missed him," I say, not saying what I feel—that Lloyd's hero never even bothered showing up.

"What a bummer," Lloyd says, looking really sad. "Why couldn't he stay longer. Didn't he know I was coming?" Lloyd grins weakly. "You better believe I'm gonna remember this. Wait until I become famous. I'll sign autographs for hours, even for you."

"You're all heart," I say. "Come on, I'll treat you to a double cone at Mr. Chocolate. You'll feel better."

"He's not even having that good of a year," Lloyd says.

I drag him out of the bookstore. "We can hang around a bit and then I gotta go see Lynne and Mr. Janowicz at the card store."

"We're gonna see Lynne? Why didn't you say so in the first place," Lloyd says, immediately brightening. "I'm beginning to feel better already."

We both pig out on mint chocolate chip cones and walk around the mall for a while. We look at some store windows, then watch a magician do some corny card tricks, and eventually wander over to the Holiday Card Shoppe. Through the front window I see Lynne straightening the cards on the racks.

"Your sister looks so cool," Lloyd says, pushing his nose up against the glass window.

"You said that before, Lloyd," I remind him.

"It proves that my love never changes," he says romantically.

"I think you got hit by the baseball instead of me," I say to him as we walk into the store.

"How much longer do you gotta wear that thing?" he asks.

"A day or so more, then I throw the patch away for good."

Inside the store are two long rows of cards broken into various sections for birthdays, anniversaries, sympathy, and so on. There's a small section for boxed candy up front and a larger section for stationery. The store is bright and cheerful looking. Music plays very softly in the background.

Lynne sees me and says, "Don't do anything stupid in here." No hello. No how are you. Typical Lynne behavior. "How you doin', Lloyd?" she says, turning toward him after dispensing with me. Lloyd melts. He has this big, goofy grin that makes him look like an idiot.

It fascinates me that anyone, even Lloyd, can find anything remotely attractive about my sister. I mean, she's pretty and all that, but she has the personality of a lemon, a stuck-up, sour lemon. I'll be walking with her, and a group of boys will turn around and whistle, and she'll pretend not to notice, but when they're gone I'll see a small smile on her lips.

"I'll be back in a few minutes or so," she says snobbishly. "Gotta get my stuff. Wait here and don't touch anything, you hear?"

"So this is the young *boychick* who stops the line drives with his eye," Mr. Janowicz says, coming out from behind the counter. "There was no damage? You can see clearly?" he asks, pointing to my patch.

"Yes, I can see," I say quietly.

"Praise God," he says, clasping his hands together.

Mr. Janowicz is a small man with a bald head, black-framed glasses, and green eyes. He wears a regular suit, a bit old looking. His body looks like a question mark, kind of slumped over. "Your sister was kind enough to keep me informed as to your medical progress." His green eyes sparkle.

"Mr. Janowicz, I'd like to thank you for getting me to the hospital so quickly," I say, remembering my mother's words. "The doctor said he was glad that more time didn't go by or things might have been worse."

Mr. Janowicz smiles, removes his glasses, and says, "My boy, what's to thank? I should leave you on the streets bleeding? This I don't do."

"But you didn't know who I was."

"It matters? Because I don't know you I should maybe forget you were hurt? A person is a person; you were hurt. That's all that counts. However, Mr. Baseball Player, it so happens I *did* know it was you. Your good friend told me your last name. I recognize it at an instant, same as your sister. Such a nice girl."

He turns his smile toward Lloyd. "So this is the young man who hit the ball. What a powerful ball."

Lloyd nods his head guiltily.

"Such an accident," Mr. Janowicz says sympathetically. "These things happen. You were not to blame. In fact, you were very helpful to me in the ambulance, very helpful."

He continues to smile at us. I feel a bit embarrassed. What's taking Lynne so long? I think.

"Baseball is truly wonderful American game," Mr. Janowicz suddenly says.

"You like baseball?" Lloyd asks in surprise.

"I watch it every chance. When I come to America after the war, I go to all the games, but now not as much as before," he says to Lloyd. Then he asks me, "When do you play baseball again?"

"I don't think my parents would let me play with this," I point to my eye.

"No, I mean after the patch comes off. You must play soon."

"Why?" I ask.

"*Tatelah*, if you don't play soon, you won't want to play the game again. Tell you something. When I was a boy, oh this was so long ago, I was playing soccer and this big galoot tackled me and I fell on the ground so hard my teeth shook in my head. My father picked me up and told me to play some more."

"Didn't he know you were hurt?" Lloyd says, interested.

"More important I should play right away, he said. Now I think he was right. I think you should play as soon as you are able. Is like falling off a horse—the rider falls and then he does not wish to ride anymore. A mistake."

A customer comes up to the register. Mr. Janowicz rings up the sale in a few seconds and then continues,

"I do not wish to go against parents' wishes, but you must play soon. You must never be afraid of anything."

"I'll think about it," I say, not really knowing what to think. I know he's right about the horse part, but my parents would go absolutely berserk if I mentioned the word *baseball* right now.

"I'll go get Lynne," Lloyd says. "Maybe I'll ask her for a date."

"Sure, Lloyd, right away. Ask her out to the prom," I say, ribbing him.

Mr. Janowicz starts to pull down a few shades. "Once, in 1948, when I first come to this country, right after the war, I had the honor to watch Joe DiMaggio play. Do you know from Joe DiMaggio?"

I nod my head. Lloyd has some baseball books on him.

"He was hurt during that year, but he played with injury. He played magnificently, like a prince, no like a king. No one knew what pain he was in. There was a time when he signed autographs for hours for all the children and he had just finished a most difficult game."

My mind flows back to the Lion and his no-show.

As if reading my mind, Mr. Janowicz says, "Modern ballplayers don't know anything, just the money."

Lloyd finally returns with my sister. "What did you

two do back there?" I tease. Lynne ignores the comment and says, "Are you still botherin' Mr. J.? I could hear you all the way in the back."

"We were talkin' about baseball. I wasn't botherin' him," I say in defense.

"They were just listening to an old man," Mr. Janowicz says kindly.

"Come on, creepo, let's go—you too, Lloyd." Lloyd breaks into a beautiful smile. "I suppose I have to drive you home, too," she says to him. I can tell by her voice that she is not too angry. "Good-bye, Mr. J.," she calls out.

"Good-bye," he says, waving his hand. "You go now, I close up."

"You sure?" Lynne asks. "We could stay."

"How you say?—'no problem.' What's to worry?"

When we get out to the parking lot behind the mall, I ask Lynne if she ate supper. "You're worried if I ate? What do you want? I don't have any money," she says.

You have to be careful how you talk to Lynne. One day she can be relatively sweet (for a lemon, that is), and the next day she's ready to jump down your throat, which is more her usual personality.

"Just talkin'," I say. "What do I care if you're a blimpazoid?"

"You're so sweet, Jeremy," she says sarcastically. "I just *love* having you for a brother."

32

I stick out my tongue at her.

"That's a mature response," she says.

We get to the car, an old Dodge Lynne bought with her savings. Lynne gets in on the driver's side. Lloyd whispers excitedly to me, "Jer, let me sit in the middle." Big thrill, I say to myself. Lloyd is so strange, especially when Lynne is around.

We ride in silence as Lloyd is content to sit next to (and sometimes stare at) Lynne. When we get to Lloyd's house, we drop him off. "Bye, champ," Lynne says sweetly to him. He sort of nods dumbly. After we get rolling again, Lynne says, "Lloyd's cute. He's gonna break hearts when he gets older."

I roll down the window to get more air. "Cut it out, Lynne," I say. "You've seen too many soap operas. That's really gross."

I'm not really mad at Lynne. This back and forth is pretty much standard stuff. The big fights we save for home, like when I mess up something in her room. I ask her about Mr. Janowicz.

"For an old guy he's pretty OK," my sister answers. "He doesn't yell at me or anything. I've never seen him yell at anyone, and believe me, we have some totally weird customers."

She stops for a light. "And my friends who have jobs? They get yelled at all the time, for lateness, for doing dumb things. Whatever. I once asked Mr. J., that's what I call him, why he never gets excited. He said, 'Enough excitement in my life. Also yelling, the soldiers all the time yelling; but that was long ago.'"

The light turns green and Lynne zooms out. "Does he have a family?" I ask.

"I don't know. I don't think so," she says, making a sharp left turn. "He never talks about it, and I never ask. Tell you something, though, he's especially nice to children. Whenever they come into the store, he's especially nice to them, even if they don't buy anything. Mr. J. is kind of odd, but I like him. I like working for him."

When we walk into the house, my mother looks up from her book and says, "Lloyd just called a minute ago. He wants you to call him back right away. Sounded important."

"We just dropped him off," Lynne says. "I wonder what he wants."

"Probably you," I say.

My sister whacks me on the shoulder.

"Something about baseball," my mother says lazily. She puts her book down. "Baseball? Good God, Jer, I hope you're not considering playing baseball again, are you?"

"It's probably not about playing baseball," I say. "Maybe he wants to tell me more stuff about Lou the Lion."

"How was that?"

"Don't ask. He wasn't even there," I say, heading

for the phone. I dial Lloyd's number. The conversation goes like this:

"Hello, Jer. What was the homework?"

"You're kidding. You didn't write it down? It was on the board."

"So sue me, I didn't write it down. I'm not used to doing work so early in the year. Takes me time to warm up. So what was it?"

"To write down our 'plan for the week'—how we spend every hour, you know, a chart."

"Can I copy yours?"

"Lloyd, are you crazy? How can you use my chart? We're two different people. Shore would know we copied."

"Guess you're right. I'll figure out something. So what do you think he meant about baseball?"

"Who said anything about baseball?"

"He did. When he was tellin' us about his life. Don't you remember?"

"Oh, yeah."

"I hope he lets us play. If the weather is too cold we could practice in the gym."

"I can't play."

"We talkin' about ability or permission?"

"So funny, Lloyd. You know my folks would kill me."

"Jer, you're all right. You told me even the doctor said so. Who knows better than a doctor? And what

about what Mr. Janowicz said about falling off a
horse? You gotta get back on the horse."

"You can play baseball on a horse? I didn't know
that."

"Stop foolin' around, Jer. You know what I mean."

"What does it matter to you if I play?"

"You think I don't feel bad you got hurt? It bothers
me."

"Why?"

"It could have been me, Jer."

A short pause and then we both start laughing real
hard.

"You're a good friend, Lloyd."

"The best you got, buddy boy, the best you got.
How's Lynne?"

"You just left her."

"See? I miss her already."

"Good night, Lloyd. I gotta go."

4

The Pep Talk

"You know, Shore's not so bad," Lloyd says out of the blue as we sit together on the school bus. It's the second week of the term, and I'm happy that I no longer have to wear my eye patch. My eye feels fine.

"Who's talkin' about him?" I say.

"I am," he says. "We just started school and we survived the first week, didn't we?"

"I guess so," I say. "But can you believe 'squads'?"

"I know, I know," Lloyd says, nodding his head. "What are you gonna do? That's the way he runs his class."

We no longer have monitors; we have "squads" —the cleanup squad, the board-erasing squad, the rexograph squad, the book distribution squad. You name it and there is a squad or detail for it. Everyone in the class is a member of at least two or three squads. It is nothing you volunteer for. You get assigned. And to top it off, medals are awarded for the most efficient and/or quickest squad. He actually times us! "Book distribution squad, twenty-one seconds—not bad," he says.

"But he's not that horrible," Lloyd continues. "You just have to get used to him. Every teacher takes some getting used to. Personally, I think you have to be a little strange to be a teacher in the first place. What normal person would want to hang around kids all day? Shore's OK."

"So far," I say. "He hasn't court-martialed anyone yet."

"Stop exaggerating, Jeremy. He's just strict. He's OK."

"OK, as long as we do what he says, as long as we do *exactly* what he says."

"What's wrong with that? He's the teacher."

"There are different kinds of teachers, Lloyd," I say. "Look what he did last week: He yelled at Cattucci for being late twice, he made Peggy feel horrible when she didn't know the answer to a math problem, and—"

"Yeah, but Peggy's not too good in math."

"What does that matter? He still made her feel bad. In gym, remember what he did to us in gym? When we were fooling around and making noise? He practically went crazy. Remember that? And what about what he did to Big Fred when—"

"Jeremy, what are you doing, keeping a list? He's allowed to do all that junk. He's the teacher. Teachers have been getting away with that stuff for years. Jeremy, you gotta go with the flow, be cool about it."

"Well, I don't like it," I say.

"Big man," Lloyd says right back. "Why don't you go right up to the front of the room and tell him?"

"I'm not stupid, Lloyd. You want me to go up against Rambo? Not me, no way."

In truth, though, it hasn't been all *that* rough. It's been tense, but as Billy once pointed out, "School ain't no summer camp."

Mr. Shore does run his class like boot camp, but we *do* learn a lot.

In class that morning, after opening exercises, the book distribution squad hands out our math workbooks "in record time," as Mr. Shore points out proudly.

Math is not my best subject, not by a long shot, and I really have to concentrate on it to keep up. Mr. Shore lectures us on the division of fractions, and by the time he hands out some practice work sheets, I think I understand how to do them. I'll say this for Mr. Shore. He does know his stuff.

After fractions, we go to assembly, where we see a dumb movie on wild animals of the North. In the afternoon (after a lunch that featured the "Splatter Platter," ground beef that looked like it wasn't quite dead yet), we continue our study of the U.S. Constitution, a "landmark document in the history of the world," as Mr. Shore calls it.

He makes us copy down a few of the first ten amendments. "The Bill of Rights," he tells us, "is the cornerstone of American freedom. It guarantees our liberties like no other document in the world."

He clears his throat for a second and then continues, "No country has ever developed so rapidly, in so many areas. I have traveled to many parts of the world, and believe me when I say that because of our drive and our competitive spirit, because of our precision and excellence, there is no country in the world that can touch us."

After history, I know we are scheduled for gym, but after last week's mess I wonder if we are going to have gym at all.

"OK, cleanup squad, take the baskets around." he says authoritatively. Maybe he'll let us have silent reading, I think.

No such luck. He tells us to line up for gym, the indoor gym.

We walk in two straight lines toward the gym.

"What's this all about?" I ask Lloyd.

"Probably about the last time we went to gym," he says.

What happened last time was a disaster, according to Mr. Shore. We were all just taking it lightly and fooling around, mostly by running and chasing each other up and down the gym, a free-for-all kind of period. Mr. Shore had been called out of the gym by a monitor and when he returned several minutes later and saw what we were doing, he became livid. "You are a reflection on me," he said when he saw us screaming all over the place. "I do not like disorder; I will not tolerate disorder," he said. He was really upset.

"We were just kidding around," Billy explained. "It was really my fault. I sort of started it."

(At that moment I thought Billy was the gutsiest person alive.)

"I am not interested in who started this fracas. As far as I'm concerned, you are all responsible, all a party to it. I do not take kindly to kidding around or general mayhem. This *will* not happen again. Believe me, this will not happen again." With that scolding over with, he spent the rest of the day in a very nasty mood.

When we get to gym, Mr. Shore commands, "Take your places."

For gym everyone has been assigned a row and place number. Mr. Shore calls these rows "patrols." I am in Patrol 3, Place 4.

We get to our places in a hurry. Mr. Shore consults the clipboard he's carrying and then begins, slowly and deliberately, "I have been quite unhappy with what I see as a decline in the moral fiber and physical fitness of our nation's youth in general and this class in particular. If last week's gym class is any indication, this class is presently lacking group harmony, cohesion, and spirit. What I saw last week was, to be perfectly blunt, pathetic. I saw children running around with no aim or purpose, literally and figuratively. What you lack is a goal, something to strive for, and it is my express intention to supply you with that very thing."

I sneak a look over at Lloyd. I have absolutely no idea what is coming, and from the look on Lloyd's face, neither does he.

Mr. Shore looks at his clipboard and then continues, his voice serious-sounding, the kind you hear on TV documentaries. "The essence of the American spirit is the drive toward victory. Nobody remembers the losers throughout the years, only the winners. The activity could be baseball, war, or life. Only the victors earn themselves a place in history."

He stops for a few seconds and then continues. "You may be one of those people who feels winning is not as important as just playing well. You are entitled, of course, to your opinion, but make no mistake. Winning is the only thing that matters to me."

"To that end," he says, his voice growing louder, "I am presenting to you my baseball plan. I can think of no better sport than baseball to show you the values I uphold, the virtues I intend to demonstrate to you, the virtues of teamwork, preparation, and spinal fortitude."

(What is "spinal fortitude," I think, a new rock group?)

Mr. Shore clears his throat and then announces, "I have cleared the following plan, which I am about to present to you, with Mr. Donovan, our principal. He thinks it's an A-one, marvelous idea, but advises me that because of socialization considerations girls are fully encouraged to participate in this endeavor, in this plan."

He pauses for effect and then says, "Some of you may know of our long-standing rivalry with Penwell Prep. I am charging you this year with upholding the honor of our school in two baseball games, one home and one away." (Lloyd lets out a cheer, but is quickly silenced by a look.) "The idea, of course, is not only to win, but to win so convincingly that they will always be afraid of us and therefore will always respect us."

"The first game with Penwell is in two weeks. I am fully cognizant of the fact that this is a very short period of time, but believe me, come game day, we will field a most credible team, one that will do our school proud. The only problem I see is that at present we do not have the necessary funds for uniforms, but I will address myself to that very shortly. Any questions?"

Peggy raises her hand. "Does everyone have to play?" she asks.

"Nobody *has* to do anything, Ms. Rigby," Mr. Shore says, looking straight at her. "But I would take it amiss if you decided that you don't even possess the necessary desire to try to be part of our team effort and determination. But of course, it is strictly your choice. Any other questions?"

After that answer everybody is afraid to say anything. "Oh, one more item of importance," Mr. Shore says. "Because the baseball field near our school is in poor shape, we will play our home game at McClaren Park and the away game at their field. I expect to see most, if not all, of you at McClaren Park tomorrow after school for our first practice. Our spirits will stand tall—on to victory. Billy, can I see you for a second? The rest of you, class dismissed."

After school Lloyd decides to come over to my house. "I'm inviting myself over. You got anything good to eat?" he says, plopping down on the living room sofa.

"Don't you have food in your house?" I ask.

"The microwave is broken. My mother brings home Chinese a lot. But tell you what, I'm in the mood for pancakes. Got any pancake mix? I'm starved."

"Didn't you eat in school?" I say.

"Who can eat that glop. I swear it was moving today."

44

"You don't think it's a little late for breakfast, then?" I point out.

"Are you kiddin'? It's never too late for eating. Stand back, Jer, and watch the master at work."

Lloyd takes the eggs and milk out of the refrigerator, and I get the pancake mix. "Where's Lynne?" he asks.

"Workin', I guess. Why? You want to invite her for pancakes?" I say.

"That's not a bad thought, Jer," he says as he mixes everything together.

"Don't you have to measure that out?" I say, referring to the mix.

"The best cooks do it by touch," he says confidently, stirring everything with a wooden spoon. "You want a big or little one? I make them to order." He pours the mixture into a frying pan, making circles of various sizes. When they get a little brown on one side, he flips them over.

As he eats his second pancake, Lloyd asks me, "You still on your first?" Even in pancakes he's gotta win. Amazing.

As he eats his third pancake, he asks me, "You gonna play tomorrow or what?"

"I'm thinking about it," I say.

"You don't think you really have a choice, do you?" he says.

"Not the way Shore was talking," I reply.

"So you're gonna play, right?"

"I'll think about it."

"I hate when you say that. You better think soon, it's tomorrow."

"I told you I'll think about it. What do you want—blood?"

"No, Jeremy, we've had enough of your blood already."

"Very cute, Lloyd."

"Seriously, Jer, you can't be afraid of a ball all your life. It was only one accident. Besides, if you don't play, or at least try out, Shore will be on your case the whole year. Believe me, I wouldn't want him on *my* case. You'll be in his permanent doghouse."

"Maybe I could just try out. That might get him off my back. I'll play far, far out in the outfield."

"Sounds good to me," Lloyd says. "I'd rather have you playing than some dumb girl. You're better than any girl we got, except Josie, that is."

"Thanks a lot," I say.

"You get the truth from me, Jer. One problem, though. How are you gonna get around your parents? Haven't they banished you for life from baseball?"

"I've been thinking about that," I say. "I think I'm gonna talk to them about horses. Yep. I'll talk to them about 'the horses.' "

5

The First Batting Practice

After school the next day we all head on over to McClaren Park. It's not terribly far from our school, but is a nice walk nevertheless. I take my baseball glove out of my book bag. "You're playing!" Lloyd says excitedly. "How did you manage that? Didn't your mom give you a hard time about it?"

"I thought I would have a really tough time convincing her," I say, pounding the glove. "But I was surprised. She said OK, practically just like that. I think what convinced her was my telling her about getting on a horse after you fall off. She understood what I meant, but she did check with Dr. Meyers."

"And your father?"

"He's still in San Francisco. I asked my mother about that, and she said she would talk to him."

"That's great!" Lloyd says. "What position are you going to play?"

"I don't know, anything but pitching, I guess. You?"

"Me? I'm pitching."

"When did you ever pitch in your life?"

"I can play any position. Don't you know that?"

Mr. Shore appears on the field just then. We hardly recognize him. He's wearing khaki sweats, a green army jacket, the kind with the letters *S-H-O-R-E* stenciled over a front pocket, and a green cap with a visor. He's carrying his clipboard, and around his neck is a silver whistle.

He blows the whistle, and we all come running around. "Do we have to get in our places?" Peggy whispers. I just look at her. What a dumb question. Mr. Shore says in a commanding voice, "OK, let's see what we have here. I know there are some pretty good athletes in this class." He actually sounds friendly. Maybe he's impressed that so many kids have showed up for practice.

He checks his clipboard and then says, "This practice will be divided into four parts—warm-ups, fielding practice, batting practice, and strategy session. We shall do this every day so that we will be fully prepared to meet and defeat Penwell Prep. I know the time is short, but what we lack in minutes, we will make up in muscle. Let's play ball, enough talk."

"I've been working on this lineup you asked me for yesterday," Billy says, pulling a piece of paper from his pocket.

"Let's see what you've got," Mr. Shore says, taking the piece of paper and attaching it to his clipboard. He reads the list: "Josie—shortstop; Jason—center field; Lloyd—catcher; Billy—first base; Cattucci—third base; Robert—pitcher; Jeremy—right field; Loretta—left field; and Lori—second base."

"Hey, how come Robert's pitchin'?" Lloyd protests. "I wanna pitch."

"We need you behind the plate," Billy says calmly. "You catch better."

"And you're batting fourth?" Lloyd adds. "Who made you king?" I can see Lloyd beginning to get very hot under the collar.

"C'mon, Lloyd, the third spot is good for you," Billy says, remaining cool. "You're fast; you get on base and then I knock you in. Simple."

"OK," Lloyd says grudgingly. He's not about to challenge Billy; you just don't do that in our class. "I'll bat third for now, but get something straight. I wanna pitch sometime soon."

"You will," Billy says, making peace.

"Hey, wait a second," Mr. Shore says, interrupting. "I'm running the show here, not you, Mr. Cisco.

I'll decide who pitches and who doesn't. Do you understand?"

"No problem," Billy answers, looking surprised.

Mr. Shore leads us through a few minutes of warm-ups, mostly running in place. In exactly fifteen minutes he tells Lloyd to get behind the plate. "Take the mask and protector from the bench over there," he says. "All the reserves get out onto the field to retrieve the ball."

We laugh. "All the reserves" consist of just Peggy and Fred. "Why do I have to get out on the field if I'm not even playing?" Peggy complains.

"Because I said so, young lady," Mr. Shore says. "Rule number one—never argue with the manager. Rule number two—go back to rule number one. Got that?"

"Yes, sir," Peggy says, sounding a bit terrified. As she runs past me out to the field, she whispers, "Jeremy, this guy is getting seriously scary."

Mr. Shore walks to the mound and says, "I am going to throw a few in. Let's see if we have any heavy-duty sluggers on this team. Everyone will get three swings. If you hit the ball, run it out for all you are worth."

Josie, up first, hits a rope over third base on the second pitch. "Good eye," Mr. Shore says. Josie smiles from first base.

"Next batter up," Mr. Shore calls out. Jason steps

up and hits a comebacker to the mound. He walks away from the plate.

Mr. Shore is on him in a second. "I said to run everything out. You never know what's going to happen on the field. The pitcher might throw the ball away; the first baseman may drop it, you never know." Then he sees Josie still standing on first. "My God, what are you doing there?" he yells, shocked. "You should have been off at the crack of the bat."

"But it's only practice," Josie says.

"I don't care if it's practice against a nursery school," Mr. Shore answers angrily. "You've got to stay awake out there—at all times."

Lloyd is up next and hits a towering short fly ball out toward Fred, who looks up and watches as the ball drops twenty feet behind him.

"What in the world are you doing out there?" Mr. Shore screams, getting red in the face. "Are your feet tied to the ground or something? Get the lead out!"

Fred doesn't say anything, but I can see the hurt look on his face. There was no need for Mr. Shore to do that to Fred. He's not an athlete. None of us are professionals out there.

Billy, up next, hits a line shot right to Peggy, who, instead of running to the ball, runs away from it. Josie and Lloyd scamper home.

Mr. Shore turns on Peggy sarcastically. "The object

of this game is to get *to* the ball, not away from it, young lady. If I wanted dodgeball players, I would have advertised for dodgeball players. This is baseball, Ms. Rigby, or haven't you noticed?"

"But I tried," Peggy says in a small voice. "The ball went too fast."

"You didn't try hard enough," Mr. Shore answers right back. "If that's trying we might as well not even bother showing up at Penwell. It would be an embarrassment. I thought there were some decent athletes in this class. Where are they?"

With Billy on third, Cattucci comes up and strikes out on three pitches. Robert follows with a ground ball up the middle, and Billy strolls home.

"Out for a walk?" Mr. Shore asks him. Not even Billy, it seems, is immune from Mr. Shore's criticism.

I'm up next. I step into the batter's box and swing wildly at the first pitch. Lloyd, from behind the plate, whispers to me, "Just meet the ball, Jer, or he'll yell at you, too."

The next pitch is inside, a ball, and I twist away, more than is needed to get out of the way. My hand goes instinctively to my eye. "The pitch wasn't even that close!" Mr. Shore shouts. "Get back in there."

I stand in. The next pitch is way out of the strike zone, and I swing and miss. The fourth pitch is right over the plate, and I take a feeble cut at it.

"You're out of there," Mr. Shore says. "Next batter."

The next batters, Loretta and Lori, both strike out.

"The bottom third of the order needs lots of work," Mr. Shore says flat out. "We're never going to win any ball games hitting like that." He calls everyone to the mound for a conference.

"Well, to put it bluntly, that was a pretty poor display of hitting, with a few notable exceptions," Mr. Shore says. "Let's see what we have on defense. The key to winning baseball is good defense. You make fewer errors than the other guy, you're going to win a lot of ball games, and winning is what it's all about, right?"

Mr. Shore walks over to the plate, takes the bat in his hand, and says, "All right, fielders, get to your positions."

When we are all ready, Mr. Shore hits a ground ball down to Josie, who scoops it up cleanly and throws it swiftly to Billy at first base.

"That's more like it," Mr. Shore says in an upbeat tone of voice. "I like what I see. I think we have a shortstop out there." Billy gets the next ground ball. He handles it flawlessly and steps on the bag. "And a first baseman, too," Mr. Shore adds, smiling. "Second base, get ready."

Mr. Shore hits a soft bouncer down to Lori. She

moves toward the ball, but it scoots under her glove.

"Whoops," Lori says.

"Try it again," Mr. Shore says.

Lori tenses her body, waiting for the next grounder. The same thing happens again as the ball rolls under her glove and stops in the outfield.

"Get down for it," Mr. Shore says heatedly. Lori looks scared. "I'm going to hit the ball to you again." He swings the bat so hard that the ball whistles toward Lori, who runs away from it this time.

"You get back to your position," Mr. Shore commands. "You're going to do it till you get it right." Lori looks like she is ready to cry.

"I want a drink of water," she says pleadingly.

"No, you stay out there," Mr. Shore says, "until you get one. Focus on the ball, on the ball, like it's the most important thing in the world. Look it into your glove. Don't quit on me now. You can do it."

We all watch, afraid to move or say anything. Again Mr. Shore hits the ball down to Lori. It bounces off her glove. She starts to run off the field.

"Freeze, young lady. Stay right there. Nobody comes off the field until I tell them to come off the field."

Lori starts to cry, but she's too afraid to run off the field. She sits down, her body shaking. Mr. Shore hits still another ground ball to her, softly this time, which bounces off her shoe.

54

This is so cruel, I think. Lori doesn't deserve this, nobody does.

"Maybe that's enough practice for her," I find myself saying to Mr. Shore. "Hit the ball to me."

Mr. Shore turns on me now. "When I want your advice, Mr. Martin, I'll ask for it. It seems to me you're hardly the ballplayer to tell me what to do."

"But you're making her cry. That's cruel."

"Be quiet. I know what I'm doing."

"It's not fair," I say, still protesting.

"Get off the field!" Mr. Shore explodes. "I'll decide what's fair. You're benched."

"Hey, you can't do that," Lloyd says, rushing in.

"What did you say?" Mr. Shore says, whipping around.

Lloyd softens. "He didn't mean that. It just came out. You can't bench him for that," Lloyd explains.

"You want to be next?" Mr. Shore says. "I'm in charge here."

Lloyd blinks. For a second I think Lloyd is going to join me on the bench. What a good friend, I think. But then Lloyd backs off and doesn't say anything.

"That's more like it," Mr. Shore says, turning his attention back to Lori. He rolls the ball to her, and she catches it just as it stops. "Good," Mr. Shore says. "You see how perseverance pays off. You can't give up on yourself when the going gets tough. You can throw the ball back in to me now. Third base, are you ready?" His voice has softened considerably.

I take my glove and leave the field. "Where do you think you're going?" I hear Mr. Shore's voice call after me.

I don't even turn around, but just keep walking—home.

6
The Designated Hitter

I get home and hear a noise, a rustling in the kitchen. "Mom?" I call.

"It's me, Jeremy," my father says.

"Dad, you're home."

"Obviously," he says. "Where's everybody?"

"I don't know," I say. "I think Lynne is working."

"I gathered that. She left a note for you. It's there on the refrigerator door. Who is Mr. J.?"

"He's Lynne's boss. How was your trip?"

He sits down at the kitchen table. "Tough, especially the flight back. We hit a couple of thunderstorms and bounced all the way from Chicago. I guess your mother's not here either. I took an earlier flight. You just getting home from school?"

"No, from baseball practice. We have a class team. Let me tell you what happened. I had a fight with my teacher who's our coach. He's gonna kill me. He's such a—"

"Later, Jeremy, I'm bushed. Wait a second, you were playing baseball—with your eye?"

"It's OK. Didn't mom tell you? The doctor said it was OK, too. He said it was nothing serious."

"Nothing serious? How can you say it was nothing serious? You don't fool around with eyes, young man. I know what your mother said; she told me about it. I don't want you playing any sports for a while."

"Don't worry," I say, thinking of how Mr. Shore benched me. "I don't think I'll be playing anything soon."

"Well, that's better," my father says, getting up and going to the refrigerator. He pours himself a glass of orange juice. "Listen, son, I've got to go and lie down. The flight took a lot out of me. Don't you have any homework to do?"

I *do* have plenty of work to do. Not that I was going to tell my father that. He'd be over me like a blanket and he wouldn't stop nagging me. Every so often he gets into one of these moods where he insists on helping me with my homework, which makes it last twice as long as necessary.

Not only does Mr. Shore give us plenty of tests, he

also wants us to hand in reports, about one a month, he says. Our current assignment is to write a report on some famous person of the revolutionary war. I know Lloyd is doing Thomas Jefferson and Cattucci is doing Benjamin Franklin. I don't know who I'm doing yet. How many guys can there be in the revolutionary war? There weren't that many people in the country at that time.

There are actually two notes on the refrigerator. The first one, which I pick up off the floor, is from my mother—"Dad will be home this evening. Clean up your room. I'll be home by suppertime."

The second note is from Lynne—"Mr. J. wants to see you this afternoon, if possible. What did you do this time, squirt?"

I've about decided to go down to the mall—who wants to do homework?—when I hear a knock at the front door and see Lloyd through the window, standing there pounding his fist into his baseball glove.

"What do you want?" I say sourly when I open the door.

"Aren't we in a great mood?" he says, stepping inside. "Where'd you run off to?"

"I should be happy he threw me off the team? What do you expect, I went home."

"You weren't thrown off. He just benched you."

"I didn't see you rushing to help me," I say angrily.

"What are you talkin' about? Didn't you see me arguing with him? I stood up for you. I told him you lost your temper."

"I didn't lose my temper. It wasn't anything like that. What he did was wrong."

"Jeremy, he's the manager. He's got the right to do anything he wants. Ballplayers have to follow orders; it's as simple as that. Listen, even Lori came back and she actually caught some balls. He set up the other positions, pretty much what Billy said. There were a lot of errors in the outfield, though. We gotta get you back playing. Then he held a strategy session. He was really into it."

"What's he doing, planning a war?"

"Seems like it. He then talked about getting a sponsor."

"A sponsor?"

"Yeah, a sponsor. He says it's too late to get full uniforms, but at least we can get jerseys with our numbers on them. He wants us to go out and find some store owners who would sponsor us, you know, anybody who likes baseball.

"Mr. Janowicz!" Lloyd says suddenly. "What a great idea! If you got Mr. Janowicz to sponsor us, I bet you'd get back to playing regularly."

"What does one thing have to do with the other?"

"Boy, are you dense. Look, do what Shore says, find

a sponsor. He'll be pleased and, presto, you'll be patrolling right field again."

"I don't know," I say. "I'll think about it."

"There's that I'll-think-about-it garbage again. Just do it."

"Maybe. I have to go down to the mall anyway. My sister left me a note."

"Did she say anything about me in the note?" he says. I give him a look. "OK, OK, just ask him about the shirts, Jer."

"I feel funny about asking him for money."

"You're not asking him for money; you're asking him to support our class. What's wrong with that? Can't you see I'm trying to help you?"

"What's the matter? You feeling guilty you didn't help me before with Shore?"

He pauses for a second and then says, "Yeah, that too."

"Start your report?" I ask him, trying to change the subject. I don't want him to feel *too* bad, only a little bad.

"Thomas Jefferson?" he says. "No way."

"I haven't even picked anyone yet."

"Listen, I gotta get goin'," he says. "Catch you later. Let me know what happens with Mr. Janowicz."

When I get to the Holiday Card Shoppe, I see Lynne at the register. The first thing she says to me is "Don't touch any cards. Your hands are filthy." So much for hello.

"Mr. J. is in the back," she says, taking a card from a customer and ringing it up. "He says for you to walk right in. He has something for you. Wouldn't tell me. Big mystery."

I pick up a card anyway, a Snoopy birthday card. "Get your hands off that," she says. "Where's your shadow?"

"Huh?" I say, putting the card back.

"Lloyd."

"Home, I guess, why?"

"No reason. Just askin'. He's sweet."

"I think he's got a crush on you."

"I know. Hurry up, don't keep Mr. J. waiting."

Behind the counter is a door. I open it and walk in. Mr. Janowicz is seated at a small desk. There are papers all around him. A table lamp with a dark green shade sits at the corner of the desk.

He looks up and smiles when he sees me. "Ah, the all-star. I'm so glad you could come. Close the door, my boy. I have something to show you."

In the middle of his desk is a large, leather-bound book filled with stamps. "Do you know what a philatelist is?" he asks.

"Isn't that someone who gives away money?" I say. I think my father once told me that.

"No," he laughs. "That is a philanthropist. I wish I could be one. No, a philatelist is one who collects stamps. Here, I wish to show these to you."

"This one is pretty," I say, pointing to a stamp with a mountain on it. "Where is Helvetia?"

"Ah so, that is another name for Switzerland, an old name. And this one here is from Bavaria. Do you know where that is?"

"No, we're only studying the United States in school."

"The world is bigger than the United States. One day I travel, yes, to all the countries in my book. Bavaria is in the southern part of Germany where I was born. I have many stamps from Bavaria. It reminds me of home."

"Do you have any relatives there?" I ask.

"Not any more. My father came from Poland when he was a young man and settled in a small town in the mountains of Bavaria. He said God give us this beautiful region. My father was a good man, yes."

"Did he collect stamps, too?"

"Did he? He had a wonderful collection. I remember. Such beautiful stamps. Many books. He was so proud of them. But they were all lost in the war, all but this one. In the school, have you studied about the war?"

"World War I?"

"No, my Jeremy, I am not so old. World War II."

"Maybe we'll get to it. Right now we're doing the American Revolution."

"Ah so, the American Revolution. I studied it; I am much impressed with it. It is important for the people to stand up to authority, no? To stand up on their own two feet. What are you studying about the American Revolution?"

"Nothing much, a little about the Constitution. We also have to make a report on famous people like Washington and Lafayette."

"Ah, Lafayette, a friend of Baron de Kalb. Did you study Baron de Kalb, no? He was such a gonif, a rascal really. He wasn't a baron, you know. He took that name for himself. His real name was Johann and he was born in Bavaria. In the mountains also. He was a great help to General Washington. Helped him in so many battles, until he was captured by the British. A brave man. I believe I have a commemorative stamp of de Kalb. Here, look. A commemorative stamp is a stamp which honors a person. Such a high honor it is."

Mr. Janowicz closes his stamp book and rubs his eyes. Then he looks at me and says softly, "Jeremy, I would like so much for you to have this book, one day soon. You will learn much by it."

"What?" I say, totally surprised.

"I want you to have it, to learn. There are a few things I wish to show you, how to put the stamps in the book, how to get, perhaps, first day covers. I will explain, but I want this book to be safe with you in the future."

"Oh, Mr. Janowicz, I couldn't. I mean, it's so valuable."

"What's money?"

"But I don't know anything about stamps."

"I said you will learn. What's to worry? You have such a quick mind; you will learn in a flash. There, it's settled."

"Don't you want to give it to anyone in your family? I mean, it's yours."

"Jeremy, there is no family. The war. I come to America with just the clothes I wore. It was very difficult, but I don't complain."

"I'm sorry," I say, not knowing what else to say.

His eyes never leave me. "You have a good heart, but I do not wish to embarrass you. There is no rush about the stamps. They won't run away, will they? I will save them for you."

I stand there feeling very embarrassed nonetheless.

"So tell me," he says brightly, changing the subject. "How is the baseball going. You play?"

I'm glad we aren't talking about the stamp book anymore. "Well, we have this class team," I begin to explain. "It's not too hot or anything. We have some good players, but mostly we're pretty bad. Our coach, he's our teacher really, wants us to practice every day for a big game coming up."

"You are not having fun?" Mr. Janowicz says. "I can tell this from your voice."

"No, not really," I admit. "Our teacher, the coach, yells at us all the time."

"This teacher yells at you in particular?"

"He benched me," I blurt out. "I said something to him because he made this girl in my class cry. He was so unfair. I told him he was wrong to do that to Lori. I can't believe I did that. I stood up to him and now I'm the one who's in big trouble."

"Describe for me what happened."

I tell him the whole story. He listens closely and then after a slight pause he says, "Jeremy, you did the right thing. You were very brave to say what you did say. You're a regular rebel, just like in the American Revolution."

I feel myself blush. Nobody has ever called me a rebel before.

"Adults can be very frightening with their orders," he says. "I know. I have seen many adults with many orders. Sometimes they wish to control everything. I have seen this."

"Even in baseball?"

"What does it matter where? Some people like to be bosses or masters. They like to control. It gives them a feeling of superiority. Happens like this."

"But this is just a baseball game."

"Little, big, makes no difference. But what is beautiful about baseball is that it does not listen to orders. It follows its own rules, no? You never know where the ball will be hit or if the fielder will catch it. Every game is different. Every score is different.

"More important than baseball is you must do what you feel in your heart is right," he continues. "This you did, and I am proud. You want me maybe to talk to this teacher? I will tell him that he is wrong to abuse his position of authority."

"Oh, don't do that. I'm already in enough trouble," I say.

"Well," Mr. Janowicz says, "then we must think if I can help you solve your problem."

Suddenly, I remember Lloyd's idea. "Maybe there is something you can help the class out with. I feel a bit funny asking you about it, though. I don't know if it's the right thing to do."

"What's to worry? Just ask it, my boy. Whatever you ask from the heart is right. Is for the class, no? I would be glad to help in any way."

"Well, we need a sponsor." I begin slowly to tell him how we could use some baseball jerseys.

"Oh, baseball shirts," he says, clapping his hands together like a child. "What an honor. I would like to do this very much. But what to write on the shirts?"

"To write?"

"Yes, the name. Your team, it has a name?"

"Oh, I'm sure anything is OK. I don't think the coach would care about any name as long as we win."

"To win is not the most important thing. Your coach needs to be reminded of that. I must tell him one day. But about the shirts, consider it done. My pleasure. I know there is a shirt place in the mall. A business friend. I will take care of everything."

"That's great. I don't know how to thank—"

"Mr. Janowicz, please come out here." Lynne's voice sounds like she is in trouble.

We both rush out of the back room, Mr. Janowicz following me. The store is empty except for two guys rifling through the cards on the racks. They each look about twenty, dressed alike in torn jeans and black shirts. The taller one is blond. There is a huge tattoo on his right forearm. The other one is shorter and skinnier and has a straggly mustache. Each of them is carrying what seems like a can in a brown paper bag. They both smell of beer.

Mr. Janowicz approaches the taller one and says, "Can I help you? But there is no drinking in the store."

"It's OK, Pops," the taller one says. "We're just looking."

"Anything in particular you are looking for?" Mr. Janowicz says, his voice stiffening. The shorter one takes a long look at Lynne, who turns away.

"Anything in particular you are looking for?" the taller one mimics. He then laughs a strange, weird laugh, takes a sip from his can, and turns to the card rack. "We're just fixin' up your cards a bit. They look a little bent outta shape."

He laughs again. There are several cards and envelopes scattered on the floor.

"Please pick up what you have dropped," Mr. Janowicz says, his voice rising just a bit.

"You mean these?" the shorter one says, dropping a couple more envelopes on the floor.

Lynne runs over and stands by me. Mr. Janowicz goes right up to the taller one and says, "I think maybe you should leave right now."

"Hold your horses, Pops. I think I gotta get a Mother's Day card. You want one, too, Buddy?" he says to his friend.

"Mother's Day was months ago," I say. Lynne puts her hand over my mouth. "Ssh," she says. I can feel her shaking, which makes me nervous.

"I want you to leave now!" Mr. Janowicz says, this time with much more emphasis.

"You tellin' us to leave? How impolite," the

shorter one says, reaching into his pocket. I think for a split second he's gonna pull out a gun. "We're payin' customers," he says, taking a crumpled bill out of his jeans and waving it in front of Mr. Janowicz's face. "You guys are always interested in money."

"I will not repeat myself again," Mr. Janowicz says to both of them. "Get out of my store now."

"Listen, Pops, you get outta my face. I don't want to have to hurt you," the taller one says, taking hold of Mr. Janowicz's shirt and pushing him back, which makes Mr. Janowicz stumble and fall. "We'll leave when we're ready. Got that, old man?"

Lynne and I stand there too scared to move. "Maybe I should get the police," I whisper. Lynne doesn't say anything. She holds on to me, too petrified to move.

We both watch Mr. Janowicz get up slowly, straighten out his shirt, and walk slowly to the front counter. He reaches in back of it and pulls out a baseball bat.

"Oh, my, he's gettin' serious," the shorter one says in mock horror. "Put that down, Pops, you'll hurt yourself. Man, I'm shaking in my boots."

"I tell you you must go now or there will be trouble," Mr. Janowicz says, walking back toward the bigger guy.

"Trouble for you, you old Jew," the tall one says. "Let me just have that stick." He makes a lunge for

70

the bat, but Mr. Janowicz sidesteps him and then swings the bat at the big man's knees. The crack that it makes sounds like a ball leaving the park for a home run. The man crumples to the floor and starts moaning while holding his knees.

The shorter, skinny man, seeing his friend on the floor and the look in Mr. Janowicz's eyes, runs out of the store.

"Now, Jeremy," Mr. Janowicz says calmly, "you go find the security guard. He should be somewhere on this floor. Try the cookie store. He's usually there. Tell him to call for a doctor."

"Are—are you all right?" I ask him.

"Me? Of course I am all right, *tatelah*. What's to worry? I should let a couple of punks walk in here and order me around? Never should I allow this."

I run and get the security guard, who has a big chocolate chip cookie in his mouth when I find him. We hurry back to the store, where the security guard calls for backup. Mr. Janowicz tells us to go home. "Is too late. Your parents will worry. I take care of things here."

"Are you sure?" Lynne asks. "We could stay."

"Is all right. You go home now."

We leave quickly and don't say a word about what happened in the store. The ride home is quick and quiet.

Just before we go into our house, Lynne makes me promise not to say a word about what happened to Mom and Dad.

When I ask her why not, she says, "If they knew they'd say that the mall was too dangerous a place and make me quit. So do me a favor and keep your mouth shut."

"What's it worth to you?" I say jokingly. "I thought it was pretty exciting."

"Yeah, that's why you looked like you were ready to pass out," she says, smiling.

Stung, I answer right back, "Me? What about you? I didn't see you rushing out there to help Mr. Janowicz."

"So I was scared, too, OK? You happy? Just keep quiet about it, will ya?"

"I never saw anyone hit another person with a bat before. Did you hear what a sound it made?"

"Ssh, not a word," Lynne says, as she puts the key in the door.

"I thought I heard the key," Mom says as we walk in. "I'm glad you're home now," she says, adjusting an earring. "We're all going out for dinner."

"McDonald's." I say.

"No, Burger King," Lynne says. "We went to McDonald's last time."

"No, real food," my mother says. "We're celebrating Dad's return. I've made reservations for Le Chateau."

"French food—yuck," we both say.

"Go get cleaned up, both of you. We're leaving in fifteen minutes." We start to go upstairs. "By the way, Lynne, how was work?"

I look at Lynne, who says, "Same old boring stuff."

7

The IntraSquad Game

"Oh somewhere in this favored land the sun is
shining bright,
The band is playing somewhere and somewhere
hearts are light;
And somewhere men are laughing and somewhere children shout,
But there is no joy in Mudville—mighty Casey
has struck out."

Mr. Shore finishes reading "Casey at the Bat." I like
the way he reads, making his voice go higher and lower
at the right moments. In reading we've been doing a
lot of sports stories this past week and a half. I think
Mr. Shore is trying to psych us up for our games with
Penwell, which are coming up soon. "Was Casey a
hero?" he asks.

"No way!" Lloyd says emphatically. "He didn't care about the team. He was just in it for himself."

"He sounds just like you," Josie interrupts.

"Shut up, Josie," Lloyd shoots right back.

Mr. Shore gives both of them a look and then asks Lloyd, "Why was that so bad as long as the goal was to win? Don't you think winning is important?"

"I do, but. . . ."

I help Lloyd out. "What does it matter if you win or lose?" I say. "There is always another game the next day, the next week, the next year, isn't there?"

"But at the end of that," Mr. Shore answers, "there is a final accounting, a clear-cut winner, a pennant race, a World Series. It is always important to know who wins; it's always important to know the score. It's like life. Predictable. The strongest teams win. Survival of the fittest extends to baseball, too."

I think about Mr. Janowicz's idea that baseball is enjoyable ("if the fielder will catch it") *just* because it's so unpredictable, but I decided not to push the point. I want to keep on Shore's better side, until I find out where I stand with the team. So every day I go on down to McClaren Park and take my place at the end of the bench.

Even though there are now only a few days to go before the game with Penwell, practice in the second week seems very sluggish. Even Mr. Shore doesn't seem his usual self. He calls the team in for a meeting.

"I don't know what's happening out there," he says, "but I've seen marshmallows move faster than you guys. Don't you realize we have an important game in just a couple of days and you're standing out there like you're waiting for a bus or something? All week long we have been practicing hard, and while I've seen some improvement, it's just not enough. We're just not good enough."

Lloyd says quickly, "It's the stupid girls' fault. They mess things up. They can't catch for nothing. We'd be a lot better if they weren't on the team. Why can't they be cheerleaders or something?"

One or two of the boys yell out, "That's right!" That encourages Lloyd to add, "Every time a ball comes to one of them, it goes right through her like a knife through butter. This is dumb. This is no way to play baseball."

Josie steps forward, goes right up to Lloyd's face, and says, "You're the one that's dumb. I seem to remember you saying the same thing about our soccer team when we played last time. You couldn't have won without us."

"Go home. This is different," Lloyd answers. "Baseball is different. Everybody knows that. Baseball requires skills girls don't have. Girls throw the ball funny—hell, they look funny."

"You're so sexist, Lloyd," Josie says angrily. "It's disgusting."

76

"You can call me all the names you want," Lloyd says coolly. "It don't change a thing. Baseball is not for girls and that's that. I don't care what Mr. Shore says we have to do."

"I can't stand you," Josie says, exploding. "I'm sick of you. All you do is put down girls all the time."

"The truth hurts, doesn't it?" Lloyd says, clenching his fist.

I look over to Mr. Shore to see if he is going to step in, but he seems to be enjoying the argument. He doesn't say anything.

"We're gonna settle this here and now," Josie declares.

"How? You gonna fight me? It'll be a wipeout—just try," Lloyd says, shaking his fist now.

"Baseball. That's how. The girls against the boys," Josie says, not backing down one inch.

"You crazy? It'll be a slaughter. That's a pathetic idea," Lloyd laughs.

"You're just chicken to play us," Josie challenges.

"But we don't have enough players."

"Stop trying to make excuses, Lloyd. You round up some guys and I'll get the girls, don't you worry. Meet you at six o'clock right here—that is, if you have the guts to show up."

"We don't need any more players," Lloyd says. "Nobody on your team can hit."

"Just be there, Lloyd. We'll see who wins."

"We'll cream you," Lloyd says.

Josie asks Mr. Shore whether he could be the umpire. "Lloyd cheats," she says pointedly.

"I did have some other things to do," Mr. Shore says, "but they can wait. A little intrasquad rivalry might be good for the competitive juices. Yes sir, it might be just the ticket to light a fire under you guys. I'll be there, you bet."

"Can Jeremy play?" Lloyd asks suddenly. "We need another good man on the field."

"Sure," Mr. Shore replies. "I certainly don't want Jeremy rusting away on the bench for life. See you later, guys, on time."

Well, I'm back playing, I think, thanks to Lloyd. But I'm not too thrilled about how I got reinstated. The boys' team just needed an extra player; Shore didn't really need *me*.

"What's this game gonna prove?" I say to Lloyd as we walk towards home. "It'll only make one side angry at the other. What good is—"

"What are you talking about?" Lloyd interrupts. "It's gonna be a friendly game. Just watch my smile as we beat the living daylights out of them."

Once more, Lloyd decides to come over to my house. "What, are you hungry again?" I say. "We're out of pancakes."

"Funny man," Lloyd replies.

When we get to my house, Lloyd disappears. I figure he's in the bathroom. I start trying to finish up my math homework. If I have time maybe I'll do some work on Baron de Kalb. I did manage to find some information on him at the local library. When Lloyd doesn't come down in a reasonable time, I go upstairs and see him standing in the middle of Lynne's room. "I smell her perfume. It's all over the place," he says. "I love it."

"Probably what you smell are her dirty clothes," I say, but that's not true. Lynne's room is superneat, with not a thing out of place. "What are you doing in here?" I say to Lloyd.

"Nothing. Just taking a survey."

"Of what?"

"Do you know your sister has ten different kinds of stuffed animals in here?" he says. "Is this a room or a zoo?"

My sister does have a weird room, which I figure reflects her personality. It has light blue walls with a matching carpet and blinds. There's an exercise bike in the corner and pink sheets on the bed. Everything on her desk and mirror vanity is neatly arranged. She immediately knows if anything is out of place, even just a little bit. Her posters of rock stars are arranged symmetrically. Even the pushpins on her corkboard are neatly lined up.

"Lloyd, get out of there," I say.

"She has," he says, counting, "a stuffed panda, a monkey, a unicorn, a rabbit, a—"

"Lloyd, get out of there! Don't touch anything. She'll kill me."

"—a snake, a dog, a lion, a dragon, a frog, and a thing of undetermined origin. What is that pink thing over there, the thing with the big nose?"

"That's Honker," I say.

"You mean these things have *names*?" he says unbelievingly. "Good God, Jer, I like your sister, but jeez, that's weird."

"Didn't you ever have a stuffed animal?" I ask. "I happen to like Honker."

"Oh, yeah, when I was little and all, but boys grow out of that stuff. What's in the box over there?" he says, pointing to a small orange case sitting on the nightstand.

"Don't touch that!" I yell, but he picks up the box anyway.

"It's her box of dead flowers. Whenever any one of her boyfriends gives her flowers, she saves the petals. I think it's kinda sick."

"I think it's beautiful," he says.

I don't know whether he's being sarcastic or not, but he gently, even lovingly, puts down the box. I grab his arm.

"I'll send her a dozen roses," Lloyd says dreamily as

I lead him downstairs. "A dozen roses when I'm a big baseball star."

The field at McClaren is pretty good, with a backstop and all, except for one area down the left field foul line known as the "Weed Patch." It's a thick clump of bushes and high grass that has never been cut down because of one very tall tree in the center of the clump that is regarded as the oldest tree around.

When we finish our homework and get to McClaren, the first person we see is Cattucci, who has brought his Labrador retriever with him.

"We're not *that* desperate for players," Lloyd says to Cat while patting Rambles on the head. The dog barks affectionately.

"He'll guard the Weed Patch," Cat says. "We can't afford to lose the one game ball we have. Watch how well I have him trained." He turns to the dog and says, "Go, boy," and Rambles trots off to left field and takes a position in front of the tall grass.

Josie jogs onto the field just then. With her are two girls I don't recognize.

"Where did you get these ringers?" Lloyd says brusquely.

"They're from the Monster class. Don't you remember them from the soccer game?"

"You can't use them," Lloyd says flatly.

"Wanna bet?" Josie replies.

"They're not from our class."

"What do you care? They're from our grade. That's good enough. Who did you want me to get—high school girls?"

The girls, Elizabeth and Michelle, look like they belong in high school. They are both, well, large.

Mr. Shore walks on over to the field just as Lloyd and Josie are about to beat each other's brains in, I think.

"We'll let Mr. Shore decide," Josie says, glaring at Lloyd.

"Everybody here?" Mr. Shore asks. "Let's get this show on the road." Josie and Lloyd both rush Mr. Shore at once, yelling about the eligibility of Elizabeth and Michelle.

Mr. Shore says, counting heads. "It makes the sides even, doesn't it—six and six, right? Let's play ball, then, a three-inning game, and I'm warning all of you, give it your best shot. I want to see a lot of hustle out there. I want to see winning baseball out there, you hear?"

Billy wins the flip of the coin and decides to have the guys bat last. The lineup has Fred and me in the outfield, Robert and Cat in the infield, Lloyd catching, and Billy pitching.

"No batter, no batter," Lloyd says as Lori steps to the plate. Billy whistles the first pitch in, and Mr. Shore calls, "Strike one." Lori swings feebly at the next two pitches and strikes out.

"What did I tell you—no team, no team," Lloyd chatters. Peggy, up next, foul tips the first pitch and watches, frozen, as the next two deliveries float over the plate. "Two up and two down, that's what we like," Lloyd sings out happily.

Josie, up third, slaps the first pitch to me in right, a clean single, which I promptly misplay into a double.

"Lucky shot!" Lloyd yells out to Josie smiling on second base. She sticks out her tongue at him. Loretta is the next person up. She taps the ball weakly to the mound, where Billy gathers it up, waits for Robert to get to the bag, and tosses it over to him for the third out.

Lloyd sums up the action of the first half inning in his best play-by-play voice: "At the end of the top half of the first, no runs, one hit, one error, and the good guys coming up."

The girls then take the field, with Josie on the mound, Lori and Peggy in the outfield, Loretta and Elizabeth in the infield, and Michelle behind the plate.

"Just hit the ball anywhere!" Lloyd yells from the sidelines. "They can't field."

But we can't hit either, as Cat, first up, goes down swinging on three straight pitches and Robert is called out on a third strike.

"She's doing something to the ball," Robert says

angrily when he walks back toward the bench.

"Yeah, she's throwin' it over the plate," Lloyd says as he steps in. Josie throws a fast ball high and tight, which makes Lloyd spin away from the plate. "Hey, what are you tryin' to do—kill me?" Lloyd yells out.

"Just movin' you off the plate," Josie answers. "It's legal."

"So you're gonna play like that?" Lloyd says.

"Like what? You started it," Josie replies, peering down toward the catcher for the next pitch.

Lloyd swings mightily at the next pitch and pops it up to Loretta, who manages to hold on to the ball after circling it. "No batter," Josie says directly to Lloyd as she trots off the field after the third out.

The game is turning into the war I knew it would. I can feel the tension all around. I wish Mr. Shore would say something, but he's definitely the wrong person to ask. I think he's enjoying all of this.

The top of the second produces nothing spectacular, except Lloyd and Josie are insulting each other openly now. Elizabeth and Michelle, and Lori hitting for the second time, go quietly in the top of the second. Billy is really pitching well, but the game is definitely not fun at all.

As Billy gets set to bat in the bottom of the second, I try to think if baseball was ever fun for me. It was once, when I was six years old and my father would bring me here to McClaren with my whiffle ball and bat. We would pitch, hit, and catch for a while. "Go out for one," my father would say as he batted the ball to me. Then he got busier at the bank, started going away on trips more. We didn't have the time together like we used to.

Billy singles sharply to left field and yells from first base, "Jeremy, move me over. Bunt." I shorten up on the bat and try to bunt, but I miss the first two pitches. Billy throws up his hands in exasperation. Knowing I can't bunt again, I dig in, trying at least to meet the ball squarely. Josie pitches me very tight inside, and I just miss being hit. There is a flash picture of an ambulance in my mind.

Lloyd calls out, "Hey, Josie, this is baseball, not target practice. Leave the kid alone." Josie ignores the comment, steps back on the rubber, winds, and throws a bullet right past me. I swing when the ball is already in the catcher's mitt.

"Oh, for God's sake," Lloyd says. "Can't anyone around here get a hit?" It certainly doesn't seem so as Fred also strikes out and Cat, up for the second time, grounds weakly to the right side, where Loretta picks up the ball and beats Cat to the bag.

In the top of the third Peggy pops it up in foul ground and Lloyd runs out from behind the plate to make a nice diving catch. With one down, Josie gets hold of a pitch and laces it into the outfield between Fred and me. The ball rolls all the way to the outfield fence.

Josie never stops running. She rounds second, turns the corner at third, and heads full speed for home. I finally get to the ball and throw it to Billy, who has come out to second for the relay. Billy whirls and then throws a perfect strike to Lloyd who seems to have it one step before Josie reaches the plate. But when Josie slides into Lloyd, the ball pops out of his glove and Mr. Shore rules Josie safe.

"I tagged her, I tagged her!" Lloyd screams.

"But you didn't have possession of the ball," Mr. Shore explains.

"She interfered with me," Lloyd argues.

"No, she didn't. Play ball," Mr. Shore answers.

Meanwhile, Josie is going crazy. "An inside-the-park home run! An inside-the-park home run!" she screams. "Whaddya mean girls can't play this game? You're not talkin' so loud now, Mr. Big Shot, are you?" she says directly to Lloyd.

Lloyd curses her out. I look to see if Mr. Shore will say anything, but he takes no notice of Lloyd's language.

Billy quickly retires the next two batters, Loretta and Elizabeth, so now it is bottom of the third, last licks.

Robert hits a comebacker to the mound for the easy

first out, and then Lloyd steps up to the batter's box. His face is red as he tenses his body. He swings wildly at the first pitch. Josie laughs at him, which only infuriates him more. Lloyd grits his teeth and ferociously swings his bat in practice. Josie then delivers a slow change-up, which Lloyd hits solidly up the middle, a line shot that almost takes Josie's head off. Josie instinctively puts up her glove, and the ball ricochets off the fingers and goes out into center field for a single.

"You did that on purpose!" Josie screams.

"Prove it," Lloyd says evenly. "The tying run is on."

Without thinking, I touch my eye, the one that was injured. If I know Lloyd, and I think I do, I'd bet he was aiming at Josie to get back at her for what she did to him the previous inning, jarring the ball loose.

Again, I look to Mr. Shore to see if he will cool things down, but he walks back to his position behind the plate without saying a word.

"Bring me in, Billy!" Lloyd yells from first base. "Let's smash them." There is no speaking to Lloyd when he gets crazy like this.

Billy then hits the first pitch, a screamer, fair, down the left field line, that takes one bounce and disappears into the Weed Patch.

Rambles, on duty, goes after the ball, finds it, and runs back on the field with the ball in his mouth. "Here, boy, bring it home," Cat calls from the bench.

Hearing the word *home*, Rambles turns and runs off the field and out of the park, still with the ball in his mouth. Billy and Lloyd cross the plate while Cat runs after Rambles.

"We win! We win!" Lloyd screams, dancing around. "Josie, you and your stupid girls lose. Whaddya say now?"

"Not so fast, buster," Josie says. "We don't lose, you do. That's a ground rule double. When a fan interferes with the ball, it's a ground rule double. Men on second and third. And since the game ball is gone, the game is over, so there. We win."

"That's not a fan, that's a dog!" Lloyd screams, going berserk. He flaps his hands like a bird flying wildly out of control.

"Same difference," Josie says calmly, her arms folded across her chest.

"That's a home run, do you hear me? A home run. Ask anyone, just ask anyone," Lloyd says, still going wild.

"We'll ask Mr. Shore," Josie says, smiling now.

Mr. Shore thinks for a second and then says, "I've never seen a play quite like this. It's one for the books, all right. But technically Josie is right. The ball was obviously interfered with so it's a double, and since we don't have a game ball anymore, I guess that's the ball game, an official ball game. The girls win."

Josie whoops in delight while Lloyd just says over

and over again, "No fair, it's a robbery!" He looks like he's going to swing at Josie. There's a crazy look in his eye. I get hold of him and pull him away. The whole game has disintegrated into a fight, or near-fight, with everybody screaming at everybody else.

Mr. Shore says above the noise, "That's what I like to see, sparks on the field, plenty of spirit. Good game, guys. Time to head on home."

I look at him and shake my head in disbelief. He's supposed to be the adult; he's supposed to know what he's doing and keep order. He's just using us to win a game for himself. I feel crummy inside.

Cat comes over and says Rambles probably went home.

Which is where I head myself.

8

The World Series—Game I

Lloyd gives Josie a dirty look as we walk into class the next day. No words are said between them, but Josie, clearly enjoying the moment, is unable to resist saying, mock sweetly, "Rambles bring back the ball yet?" Lloyd just glares at her.

After opening exercises Mr. Shore walks in front of his desk and says, "Troops, I'm beginning to like what I see on the field. Yesterday you showed me grit; you showed me you have the will to succeed, the necessary drive to win."

He pauses for a second and then continues, "Penwell is tough and fast, and from what I hear they have excellent pitching. But I know we can come away with a victory, not only in tomorrow's game, but in next week's as well. Make no mistake about it. This is our World Series—a two-game series. A split is no good. I want a sweep. What do you say?"

Lloyd yells out, "We'll kill 'em, Mr. Shore!"

"That's the spirit," Mr. Shore agrees, "especially because you're going to be the starting pitcher. Billy pitched in the intrasquad game. Besides, I want to save him for the second game. Robert can play first base; he's tall."

"I'm psyched!" Lloyd shouts happily.

Mr. Shore continues, "Before I announce the starting lineup, I've just been informed—this morning, in fact—that Jason, our center fielder, has come down with the chicken pox, so that will mean that Jeremy will play center field, with Fred moving to right. Here's the batting order we will use:

Josie—shortstop; Loretta—left field; Billy—catcher; Robert—first base; Cattucci—third base; Lori—second base; Lloyd—pitcher; Jeremy—center field; Fred—right field."

"Now let's get back to business—academic business," Mr. Shore says. "We have some history work to do."

For the rest of the morning he shows us how to set up our reports on heroes of the American Revolution. "I hope all of you are well into your research at this point," he says. He shows us a sample cover page, footnote page, and bibliography page. "This is the skeleton of your report," he says. "You now have to supply the flesh on the bones, the 'meat' of your report, so to speak. Does anyone know what a footnote is?"

Cattucci raises his hand. "It's like when a dog raises his paw and says, 'Hi,' " Cattucci says, grinning. We all groan at his silly joke.

Mr. Shore allows himself a smile, a small one, explains why a footnote is needed in a report, and then goes on to say, "Some of you might need additional background information on the war itself. I'd now like to show you these slides of famous battle sites of the American Revolution. I might add that I took these pictures myself."

He sets up the slide projector. "Lori, will you please get the lights?" he says. For the next few minutes Mr. Shore narrates the story of Bunker Hill, the Battle of Trenton, and the Battle of Saratoga. "The American victory at Saratoga was the turning point of the war. It destroyed British plans to divide the colonies and boosted Continental morale. It helped convince France to come to the aid of the American cause."

Just as the lights come back on, a monitor from the main office tells Mr. Shore to send two monitors down to the office. "Robert and Fred, you're on supply detail this week. See what this is all about," he says.

Five minutes later the boys come back lugging a pretty big carton. They plop it on Mr. Shore's desk.

"Jeremy, come up here," he says. What did I do now, I think. Mr. Shore says to me, "Since this package is addressed to the class in care of you, you better open it up."

There is no return address on the carton, I notice as I take a scissors and cut into it. Inside, wrapped in plastic envelopes, are V-necked jerseys with the name "Card-inals" in red on the front and different numbers on the back.

Everybody rushes up to the front of the room. "Jeremy, do you know who this is from?" Mr. Shore asks. "I have an idea," I say. There is an envelope with my name on it taped to the inside bottom of the carton. I tear it open and read the small script.

Dear Jeremy,

Well, here, my all-star, is what I promised you. Nice, no? Use these shirts in good health, my boy. I hope the sizes fit. I want you to have a good time on the ball field with them. I select a name for your team. I hope you do not mind my choosing. A small joke. Maybe people will see it and think of my little store.

With much affection,
Mr. Josef Janowicz

P.S.   I will see if I can come and watch you play. It would give me great pleasure to

93

do this. Perhaps Lynne will be so kind as
to accompany me. She says she wishes to
watch her two favorite all-stars play.
Enjoy the shirts.

Mr. Shore gives me a questioning look.

"Mr. Janowicz is my sister's boss down at the card store in the mall," I explain. "She's also being sarcastic."

"Your sister's being wonderful," Lloyd says, looking over my shoulder. "I'm gonna hit two home runs for her."

Mr. Shore says to me, "Jeremy, you came through for us. This is great for team morale. Mr. Janowicz sounds like quite a character. I look forward to seeing him at the game and personally thanking him for his generosity."

"Jeremy, you got us uniforms!" Billy yells out. "Well, technically, half uniforms, but way to go. Not only are we good, we're gonna look good, too."

We spend what time is left before lunch trying on jerseys over our shirts and swapping them for the right size and our favorite numbers.

His first name is Josef, I think to myself. I didn't even know that.

Lynne is home watching a soap opera in her room when I return from school and a short practice in the afternoon. "Aren't you working today?" I ask her.

Still watching the screen, she says, "No, dodo brain, I don't work every day, don't you know that? Three days a week, that's all. I'm working tomorrow. By the way, what were you doing in my room yesterday?"

"How could you tell—" I start to say.

"My stuffed animals were out of line."

"Lloyd wanted to see your room. We didn't break anything, honest. He said he could smell your presence in the room."

"You mean my perfume."

"That too."

"Well understand something—my room is off limits to you and your friends, even Lloyd, got that?"

To change the subject, I tell her the story of Mr. Janowicz's generosity. She is impressed for all of ten seconds before her soap opera claims her again.

"See you later," I say to her.

"Where are you going?" she says into the screen.

"Down to the mall," I say. "I gotta see Mr. Janowicz."

"Will you stop botherin' him?" she says, still not looking at me.

"Botherin' him? I'm not botherin' him," I say. "He likes me and I like him."

When I get to the card shop and personally thank Mr. Janowicz for the shirts, he says, smiling, "What's to thank? A simple matter to arrange. I wish to do this, so I do it. Now in my life I do what I want, not what others tell me to do. When is the big game, did you tell me?"

"Tomorrow," I say, "and I'm playing."

"Wonderful! And the shirts were there on time. I was worried about this."

"Thank you again," I say.

He waves his hand. "So listen, maybe you come to look at some new stamps. I want to show you something I just got. You can call home and tell them you'll be late for dinner. I go get the stamps," he says, his voice brightening. "You make your call and watch the store for a minute. A customer comes to buy something, you just look at the price and ring it up." He sees my worried look. "What's to worry? You can do it. You will be—how you say?—a 'natural.'"

In about one second I feel five years older, like I'm a grown-up or something. I feel even better when someone comes into the store and buys a birthday card. I ring up the sale and give the lady her change. "Have a nice day," I say.

With my mother's permission I stay in the store till closing time. Not that many customers come in, so Mr. Janowitz and I have plenty of time to go over his stamps. He tells me about the countries the stamps are from. He knows so much.

"Do you show this book to other people?" I ask.

"There is no one else, really. Once, yes, not now," he says softly. "Now I live alone."

I want to ask him what he means by "once, yes," but I feel funny about asking him any more about his life. I don't know quite how to explain it, but his life feels very scary to me. He sees me staring blankly at him.

"Come, let me tell you about Sierra Leone," he says, turning a page. "A West African country. See how interesting this stamp is. Is in the form of the country, the outline. Sierra Leone was first to do this. Interesting, no?"

Just before he closes the store, I ask him if he really wants to come to our game with Penwell. "It's not that big of a deal," I say.

"Oh, but it is," he says. "I wouldn't miss it for the world."

The next day, game day, gives me the jitters—so bad, in fact, that the butterflies in my stomach are setting distance and speed records.

"The time for talk is over," Mr. Shore says at the end of the school day. "Zero hour approaches, and we are ready to meet our foes. At least I hope we are ready."

"What time did you say Lynne will get to the game?" Lloyd says to me as we walk toward McClaren Park.

We very quickly get to McClaren and walk toward the field. Two Penwell buses are already in the parking lot—gleaming coaches, the kind that have bathrooms in the back. The Penwell Panthers, as they are called, look professional. We see them warming up on the field. They have regular uniforms that are black and yellow and awesome. Even with Mr. Janowicz's jerseys, we look like a pickup team. If the Panthers play half as good as they look, we are in for a very long afternoon. They even have their own cheerleaders with them, who are already leading a small group of parents in a cheer. We don't even have Rambles.

During batting practice I look around for any sign of Mr. Janowicz, but I don't see him. Maybe he couldn't get away from the store.

"Did you see Lynne?" Lloyd asks.

"Aren't you supposed to warm up? You're pitching, you know."

"In a sec. Is she here?"

"I don't see her," I say.

"My heart is broken," he says. The funny thing is that I think he means it.

"Lloyd, the mound?"

While Lloyd trots out to the rubber, Penwell's coach walks past me and over to shake Mr. Shore's hand. "What's the matter, Mark" their coach says, "you couldn't get enough boys to play?"

"Just get on the field, Gene, and we'll see who's better," Mr. Shore says, annoyed.

"Are you kidding?" the Penwell coach answers.

"They look ready for jump rope, not baseball. This is a joke, right? Where are you keeping the real players?"

Mr. Shore gives him a dirty look, but the Penwell coach continues.

"I didn't think you'd ever risk being on a losing team again, Mark." Then with a mocking smile, he adds, "We all know how you get when things don't go your way. . . ."

"We'll kill you," Mr. Shore says heatedly.

"Hey, no offense, Mark," their coach says. "I was only kidding."

"Sure, right," Mr. Shore says angrily. "Just get your first batter up there."

Since McClaren is our "home" field, Penwell gets to bat first. Lloyd finishes his warm-up pitches and gets ready to face the leadoff batter.

Before he delivers the first pitch, he turns around toward me in center and flashes an OK sign with his hand.

The leadoff hitter hits a hard shot to Fred in right, who blocks the ball with his body. Before Fred can get a handle on it, the Penwell batter has reached third.

Lloyd screams at Fred, "What a dumb error!" Mr. Shore yells at Lloyd for laying the ball right in there. But the loudest yell belongs to Fred because the ball skipped up and hit him in the chest.

Mr. Shore rushes out to the mound to speak to Lloyd, who hangs his head for a second. I can't make out what Mr. Shore is saying, but whatever was said, was not effective, as Penwell's second batter whacks the ball into the gap between me and Loretta for a double. The game is barely one minute old and already we're losing.

Again, I look around for Mr. Janowicz and Lynne, but I don't see them. In a way I'm glad. From the way this game is starting, I'm getting the distinct feeling that we are going to be beaten very, very badly.

I wish I can say I am wrong, but I'm not, as the first six batters reach base safely with four runs already in. Josie saves us from further destruction with a nice stop of a line drive. Lloyd manages to strike out one weak batter, and another is retired on a pop-up foul ball, which Billy spears.

In the dugout Mr. Shore lets out his frustration on everyone. "You call that pitching? You call that fielding?" he says angrily. "I thought you could pitch," he says directly to Lloyd. "What happened out there?"

"I don't know," Lloyd says almost in a whisper.

"Well you better find out because I'm leaving you in," Mr. Shore says. "I can't bring Billy in, and nobody else can pitch. So next inning be sharp if you don't want to further embarrass yourself."

Josie offers to pitch, but Mr. Shore is so upset he waves his hand in disgust. "If I take you out of the infield, we'll have nobody who can catch a ball. You stay put." Josie shrugs her shoulders. To the rest of us Mr. Shore says, "Let's see if we have any hits in our bats. Let's go, it's early. We spotted them enough runs. We can do it!"

It's not early enough, as our batters don't help Lloyd out too much in the home half of the inning. Spencer, the Penwell pitcher, stares into McDaniels, their catcher, for the sign. But before he delivers he straightens and yells, "A girl leading off—they must be hard up!"

This makes Josie so angry she swings wildly and misses three straight pitches by a mile. Loretta doesn't even get the bat off her shoulders as she is called out on strikes, and Billy manages to foul off one pitch before he taps a weak roller to the first baseman, who makes the play unassisted.

While Billy is up at the plate, I turn to Lloyd in the dugout and try to cheer him up. "So it won't be a pitcher's duel," I say. "We'll get 'em."

Lloyd looks over to me sadly. "I stink!" he says. That's all he says.

"Come on, Lloyd. There's still time to get them," I say.

"Shut up, Jeremy," he says angrily. "Just leave me alone. Leave me alone, will ya?"

"OK, OK," I say, backing off.

The next inning is only slightly better. We give up

two runs in the top of the second on three base hits and two errors.

Still Shore doesn't take Lloyd out. (Why doesn't he, I think.)

In our half of the second we don't go down one-two-three, as Robert walks and Cattucci gets on base on an error by their third baseman. For a brief second I have hopes of a huge rally, even after Lori strikes out and Lloyd steps up to the plate. But that idea goes by the boards as Lloyd, trying too hard, goes down swinging on three pitches.

Mr. Shore is pretty uptight. "We can't hit, we can't field, what can we do?" he asks in exasperation. Lloyd passes me as I walk up to the plate. "Close game," he says sarcastically. I smile thinly. "Just call me Casey," he says, walking back to the dugout.

"What have we got here?" McDaniels, their catcher, says as I step in. "No ballplayer, no ballplayer."

Obviously, he's right, as I don't swing anywhere near the ball.

To describe the rest of the game would be cruel and inhuman punishment. It's like one of those horrible nightmares you have when someone is always falling or something is always out of reach. I contribute a couple of errors to the game as well, but I don't feel too miserable since everyone else is playing lousy, too.

The game is like when TV sports reporters do their "Plays of the Month," which are supposed to be funny but are really embarrassing. Especially if you're part of the film.

Roll 'em.

• Fred tries to throw a ball back into the infield, but it slips out of his hand and falls behind him.

• Robert swings at a pitch. The bat flies out of his hands and goes farther than practically any ball we've hit all day.

• A bouncing ball to Cat at third goes through his legs. Cat looks between his legs and falls down.

• Lori catches a ground ball and, for some strange reason thinking it's a force play, tosses it to second, but no one is there, fielder or runner.

In the top of the sixth with the score 12-0, we are all just waiting to go home. I look over to Mr. Shore, who is not saying much of anything anymore. He stands sort of slumped against the dugout wall, staring out, glassy-eyed, at the field. I look for Lloyd, but don't see him anywhere. I wonder where he is. I ask some of the guys, and Cat says Lloyd mumbled something about sitting out behind the Weed Patch. It's our last licks, but it doesn't take a genius to figure out that the game is totally out of reach.

I don't know why, but something feels wrong. I slip away from Mr. Shore and head for the Weed Patch myself. I'm worried; maybe Lloyd hurt his arm pitching so much.

I see Lloyd sitting on an old log behind the Weed

Patch, his face in his arms. I go up and tap him gently. "Lloyd, you OK?" From where he's sitting you can't see the field at all.

He looks up. He's been crying. You don't need a detective to figure that out.

"Yeah, I'm OK," he says, wiping his face with his sleeve.

"I don't feel like going back to the game either," I say, sitting down next to him. We both sit there quietly for a few minutes. Lloyd says only one thing. "Lynne wasn't at the game, was she?"

I shake my head no.

We sit there for I don't know how long until Mr. Shore finds us. He chews us both out for leaving, but he's not so intense about it.

Walking out of the park he says to the team, "We'll have to regroup; we'll have to fight back. You lost your spirit out there and made physical and mental errors. This doesn't have to happen again."

When I get home, I slog through the door and head up the stairs toward my room. The only thing I want to do is take a hot shower and wash away all thoughts about the game.

My mother stops me as I'm halfway up the stairs. "Jeremy, come down," she says.

"What's wrong?" I ask, suddenly alert to an eerie quiet in the house. Lynne is sitting on the sofa, very upset. Her makeup is all messed up, I notice.

104

"It's Mr. Janowicz," my mother says. "He's in the hospital, a heart attack. Lynne had to call the ambulance."

"Is he OK?" I ask. I feel my stomach tightening.

"Well, it's not critical, but it's serious enough. Anything at his age is serious."

"Is he gonna die?"

"I don't think so."

"I wanna go see him."

"Not now," my mother says gently. "Maybe in a few days. I don't think it's too bad, but for now we'll just have to wait and see what happens."

I go over to the sofa and sit next to Lynne. She reaches for my hand. "Oh, Jeremy, it was so awful. I didn't know what to do. He was trying to keep *me* calm."

We sit there for a long while. I do not even mention the ball game. Now, at this moment, our embarrassing loss to Penwell seems very far away and no longer very important.

9

The Disabled List

The next day, Saturday, is no school and I sleep late. When I wake up at eleven, I put on my pair of jeans and a T-shirt and go downstairs for some Rice Krispies. The day matches my mood—gray and rainy.

"Well, what are you going to do today, sleepyhead?" my mother asks as I stare into my bowl of cereal.

"I don't know," I say quietly.

"You OK?" my mother says. "Look at me. I don't like the way you look."

"I'm OK."

My mother stirs her coffee. "Well, you don't sound it," she says.

"I want to see him."

"Who?"

"Mr. Janowicz. Who do you think I mean?"

"You can't, not now at least."

"Why can't I? He took care of me when I was in the hospital, didn't he?"

"Jeremy, it's not the same thing. I know you feel bad for him, but the doctors are taking care of him. In fact, the doctor I spoke to this morning said it wasn't that serious, thank God. I'm sure he'll be all right, and I'm sure you'll get the chance to see him soon.

Lloyd comes over later in the day and we sort of hang around. He walks up and down my room, unable to sit down. "You want to play Monopoly or Scrabble?" I suggest.

"Those stupid games?" he says. "Monopoly takes forever, and I can never spell the words I want to put down in Scrabble."

I tell him about Mr. Janowicz.

"That's a bummer," he says. "Is he gonna be all right?"

"My mom thinks so. I'd like to see him. You wanna come?"

"Me? I hate hospitals. I'll see him when he gets out. I feel depressed enough."

"You still upset about the game?"

"Naah, not really. It was only one game. We still got another shot at them."

"After 12-0? Are you kidding?"

"They're not that good, trust me. They got a lot of cheap hits."

"I wonder if Mr. Shore is still mad at us."

"He was mad at me mainly," Lloyd says. "I stunk the place out. He had a right to yell at me; he's the manager, right?"

"He didn't have the right to torture you," I point out. "He could have pulled you out for a relief pitcher."

"Yeah? Who could have pitched?" Lloyd challenges.

"Me," I say.

"You? Get real. Jeremy. You had trouble hitting the handball wall. Knock it off. You wanna go bike riding?"

"In the rain?"

"Why not? You won't rust, Jer."

We go bike riding while it's drizzling. It feels refreshing.

On Monday in school I expect Mr. Shore to really tear into us, but he doesn't. After morning exercises he says simply and quietly, "We were badly beaten. That's all there is to it. But adversity makes one stronger, braver. It tests our mettle. We will regroup our forces and take it to them."

I look at Lloyd in surprise.

No ranting.

No yelling.

No abuse.

"One more thing," he adds. "I have rescheduled our game for a week later. This will give us an extra week of practice, time to get back to basics. We will work very hard, very hard indeed. Then we will be able not only to avoid humiliation—make no mistake about it, we were humiliated—but we will be in a position to seize victory. Count on it."

The rest of the morning we spend on the American Revolution, on the problems facing the new nation. The only reference Mr. Shore makes to baseball is when he says at one point, "Everything worthwhile is a struggle, not without defeats and setbacks, whether it be an emerging country or an emerging ball team."

He reminds us that our written reports are due by the end of the week and that he will give us extra credit if they are verbally presented. I shrink in my seat. He doesn't have to know that I've only done about half the research.

Loretta raises her hand like a shot. "What I want to know, Mr. Shore, is whether I can read my report on Martha Washington in class?" she asks. "It's so good."

Yeah, like her report a couple of years ago on the Apaches, I think. It was so long. Loretta will probably grow up and make boring reports for companies or something like that. But not before she tells a few amusing stories or jokes.

After school we practice long and hard. Mr. Shore

concentrates on fundamentals like hitting and catching. He hits countless balls down to us at various positions. I come home fairly exhausted. He puts us through the same routine on Tuesday as well.

When I come home from school and a particularly tough practice on Wednesday, my mother says to me, "He asked for you."

"Who's that?"

"Mr. Janowicz. He's a lot better now and well on the highway to recovery. That's what he said. I think he meant the road to recovery."

"You spoke to him? How is he?"

"I just told you."

"When can I see him?"

"I wrote down the visiting hours on the pad there. Apparently he wants to see you right away. Why don't you go with Lynne?"

"No chance. I asked her about that yesterday. She says hospitals give her the creeps. Lloyd said the same thing. I better go myself. Don't worry, I'm not that tired."

"Give him my best, then," my mother says as I look on the pad and see that the hospital has afternoon visiting hours. "Give him my very best."

When I get to the hospital, I go to the admissions desk and ask for Mr. Janowicz's room and get sent to a nursing station on the fourth floor. The nurse behind the counter says coldly, "Can I help you?"

110

I tell her my first name and ask to see Mr. Janowicz. She disappears around a corner. In a few minutes she comes back and says more kindly than I expect, "Your grandfather will see you now. Don't stay too long, only a few minutes, and don't talk about anything that would upset him."

I just nod and follow her on tiptoes around the corner. The hospital is so quiet, I feel like I have to whisper.

I enter the room and see Mr. Janowicz sitting up in a corner bed. He turns and smiles radiantly. "So now you are my grandson. I have made it official. Otherwise they would not allow me the pleasure of your company. You do not mind?"

"Of—of course not," I say. I do not know what to say next.

He sees my discomfort. "These machines, they bother you, don't they?" he says, referring to the monitor above his head. "A real miracle worker."

"How are you feeling," I finally manage to get out.

"How am I feeling? I am good as expected can be. Quite good, in fact. What's to worry? I don't complain. It could have been worse. More important, how was your big game? Was it fun?"

"We lost, we lost badly," I say without enthusiasm. All those machines and monitors do frighten me. They appear much more menacing than they do on TV.

"You do not answer my question. Not important

won or lost. To me matters if the game was exciting. Was it?"

"Not very," I say hesitatingly. "It was a blowout."

"What means 'blowout'? Explain to me in detail."

I describe the game in full to him—all about Lloyd's pitching, Penwell's batting, and our miserable fielding. Mr. Janowicz listens carefully and then says, "Such are the fortunes of baseball, happens like this. Even the Yankee Clipper, DiMaggio, had his bad games, no? I am only sorry I was not there to root you on. Next game, I come, I promise. So tell me, your teacher lets you play?"

"Yes," I say. I also tell him how upset Mr. Shore got at all of us.

"This is a difficult man, a very troubled man I think, one what lets himself get carried away with his own anger. No good for the children to see this. I talk to him," Mr. Janowicz says, getting agitated.

"Oh, please, Mr. Janowicz, don't do that. Forget about it, it's nothing," I say, remembering what the nurse said about not upsetting him.

"So tell me," he says after a nurse comes in to check his pulse and quickly leaves. "You did not mind wearing my shirts?" he says more calmly.

"You mean our uniforms? Mind? It was wonderful. I think the name you chose was great—the Cardinals."

Mr. Janowicz motions me closer with his finger.

112

"Now, I want to show you something. Look in the first drawer." He points to a little table that is next to his bed.

I pull out his leather-bound book of stamps and look at him in surprise. "When the ambulance come," he explains, "I tell Lynne to get the book. I do not wish to leave it behind. Let me see the book now."

I hand it to him, and he turns a few pages. "Ach, such beautiful countries. Did I tell you I wish to visit every one of them?"

"When you get better you can still go," I say hopefully.

"From your lips to God's ear," he says. "Yes, it is still possible. If God allows." He closes the book and hands it to me. "I want you to keep the book," he says suddenly.

"Oh, I couldn't—," I start to say.

"Until I get better. To tell you the truth, it makes no sense for the book to just lie in the drawer. You will learn much from it. It would make me happy. There is no one else."

"No one?" I say dumbly.

"It was the last thing my father give to me before they took him away. In the war this happened. Happened to many people like this. We were hiding in a barn in the mountains. A brave family, Gentiles, let us stay there. At great risk, I don't have to tell you. Even with the animals on the farm there was little food. So once my father went out to try to find some. I did not see him ever again."

Mr. Janowicz catches his breath and then continues. "Later we heard he was captured in the town by the Nazis. He did not tell them where we were hiding. He was such a good man. My mother loved him so, and she died soon after. Of disease. There was no medicine."

He wipes his forehead with the back of his hand and looks at me with a smile. "So you see, I wish to put this book in—how you say?—good hands."

What about his own wife, his own children, I think. I want to ask what happened to them. (Did he ever have a wife and family? I don't know.) But I am too embarrassed to ask. He has told me so much. He has given me so much. What have I given him?

As if he were reading my mind, he says, "Jeremy, what are you thinking about? That the company of an old man is not exciting? No? Next time you see me I will be much improved, much better. We will discuss what you have learned from the stamps. Your visit cheered me up, more than you can imagine."

Still not knowing exactly what to say, I step closer to him, take his hand, which is on the white sheet, and squeeze it gently. He nods and says quietly, "Give my love to your wonderful family. Tell Lynne I give to her a call when I open the store again. Good boy, my Jeremy. I see you soon, no?"

"Take care of yourself, Mr. Janowicz," I say as I see the nurse at the door motioning to me that my visiting time is up.

"What's to worry? I have no complaints," he says, waving as I walk out of the door. "I am alive, a survivor, no?"

Over the next two weeks in school, there is no miracle, no sudden change from a team that got whipped 12-0 into a superpowerhouse, no electrifying speeches from Mr. Shore that transforms us into baseball terrors. We are basically the same bunch of guys making slight improvements in our game. We notice as we make fewer errors, fewer strikeouts, and fewer mental errors.

We'd settle for a small miracle, a little bit of luck here, a skillful play there. We could use a bona fide hero, a Joe DiMaggio, someone who could give us a shot, to lift us to the point where we wouldn't embarrass ourselves again.

And in our practice sessions every afternoon, a little fortune does smile on us. We find a small ray of hope, a light right in our group. The ray of light is Billy Cisco.

It happens this way.

After Lloyd was shelled so mercilessly, nobody really wanted to get on the mound, not even Billy, who, though slated to pitch in the second game, was reluctant to be target practice for the Penwell batters.

115

In the second week of our practice, Wednesday, I believe, Cat is trying his hand at pitching. He doesn't get within four feet of the strike zone. Billy, playing third base for the day, all of a sudden throws down his glove and declares, "I'm tired of all this bull. Cat, get over to third and give me that stupid ball."

"Gladly," Cat says gratefully.

And though Billy never really pitched before in a regulation game, he zings the ball over the plate. The ten or so pitches he throws are all around the strike zone.

For the moment Mr. Shore is pleased. I see his first smile in a week as he says, "Platoon, I think we have found ourselves a starting pitcher."

For the two weeks Mr. Shore drives us hard with lots of fungoes—pop-ups, line drives, fly balls, ground balls, everything. He never goes crazy; he doesn't yell, but bubbles inside like a teapot. He grits his teeth, pounds his fist, and throws up his hands as he urges us to run harder, jump higher, and throw farther.

We wait for him to explode, go berserk, but he controls himself. Our practices are tense, but they are getting productive.

Loretta tries to reduce the tension by yelling out jokes from her fielding position, silly jokes like: How do you make a strawberry shake? Answer: Take it to a scary movie. Mr. Shore's grim face cuts her off before she really gets rolling into her comedy routine.

116

At the end of two weeks we are definitely catching better and making more contact with our bats.

At night I am so tired from practice that I keep postponing my homework. The one nice thing that Mr. Shore does is postpone the due date for our revolutionary war paper till after our game with Penwell. He actually gives us a compliment. "You troops have been working so hard that an extension on your reports is very much in order. Be advised that said reports will be due exactly seventy-two hours" (three days, I think fast) "after our win over Penwell."

Even with the extension I am still way behind.

The best news of these two weeks is far more wonderful than any extension. Mr. Janowicz is much better, so much better that he is now home from the hospital, resting. I speak with him four or five times on the phone, and he always sounds so glad to hear from me. We talk about baseball and stamps mainly. I tell him about our practice sessions and ask him questions about certain countries and their stamps. (I did go to the school library to get a book on stamps.)

Mr. Janowicz always ends our telephone conversations with "Such a wonderful boy you are, a mensch, really." It always embarrasses me to hear him say that, but I like his saying it anyway.

10

The World Series—Game 2

Exactly two weeks after our humiliating defeat, we walk through the gates of Penwell Prep and up a long, winding road. The buildings are brick red, some of them sprinkled with ivy. On the top of the main building is a white bell tower, which chimes four times as we head toward their ball field.

"Wish we had a field like this," Cat says, awestruck as he stares at the professional-looking diamond. The green grass, cut short and perfect, glistens in the afternoon sun. The foul lines stretch out white and straight and extend to an even six-foot fence. No Weed Patch here.

The Penwell cheerleaders, very flashy in their bright yellow and black uniforms, are already in place as we look around. A small group of trumpets and a bass drum greet us as we collect our stuff and head on over to the field.

Lloyd suddenly punches me in the shoulder. His mouth opens, but no words come out. He points to a taxicab that has just discharged its passengers.

"My God, it's, it's Lynne," he stammers. "She came to my game. Fantastic!"

"And Mr. Janowicz, too," I say.

We run over to both of them. Mr. Janowicz is dressed in his usual business suit, but on his head is a bright red baseball cap. Lynne, too, wears a baseball cap and looks good (for her, I think) in a leather skirt and matching blazer. Mr. Janowicz walks slowly with a cane, with Lynne supporting him at the elbow.

"Mr. Janowicz, you look great," I say excitedly.

"Lynne, you look great," Lloyd says, even more excitedly.

"Can I take your arm?" I say to Mr. Janowicz.

"Can I take your arm?" Lloyd says to Lynne.

We all laugh. Mr. Janowicz gives me a big hug and Lynne says, "What the heck," and gives Lloyd a hug, too.

Then Mr. Janowicz says, "So you see I am here. As promised. Surprised? So am I. Lynne was kind enough to help me, a wonderful girl, this sister of yours. My doctor was not sure this idea to see a baseball game was good. I tell him I must go anyway, with or without his permission. I insist to come."

119

"I hope I don't embarrass you," I say.

"You, *tatelah*, never," he says.

"I'm gonna hit a homer for you," Lloyd says dumbly to Lynne.

"That's so sweet of you," she says, smiling at him. Lloyd looks like a lovesick poodle. I'm beginning to get ill.

"So show me this coach that yells," Mr. Janowicz says with good humor. "I like to meet him."

I run over to get Mr. Shore who's talking to the Penwell coach. At first I thought that Mr. Shore might be too busy to meet Mr. Janowicz, but he follows me over to where Mr. Janowicz and Lynne are standing.

"So glad to meet you, sir," Mr. Shore says, extending his hand.

"And this is Jeremy's sister, Lynne," Mr. Janowicz says, politely formal. He nods his head slightly.

"Glad to meet you too, miss," Mr. Shore says. Then turning back to Mr. Janowicz, Mr. Shore says, "I really wish to thank you for the jerseys, for your generosity. Those jerseys were first-rate."

"You wish to thank me?" Mr. Janowicz says, arching his eyebrow. "There is no need. But let me explain something to you. In German there is—how you say?—an expression, '*Alles fur die Kinder.*' It means this: Everything for the children. You would agree, no?"

I feel Mr. Janowicz is saying something to Mr. Shore

120

that I don't quite get. Mr. Shore blinks once and says, "Oh, definitely. These ballplayers are special here, all right. Make no mistake."

Mr. Janowicz fixes him with a stare and says solemnly, "All children are."

"Er—yes," Mr. Shore says, hesitatingly, then recovers and escorts Mr. Janowicz and Lynne to two chairs just beside the dugout. "You can sit here; you're our special guests," Mr. Shore says gallantly. I can tell by Lynne's expression she thinks Mr. Shore is so cool.

Lloyd and I go sit in the dugout. On the bench Lloyd punches my shoulder again. "Jeremy, help me out," he says frantically. "What did I say? I promised I'd hit a home run for Lynne. What a dumb thing to say. She'll think I'm an idiot."

"She'll think what everybody already knows, Lloyd," I say, giving him the needle. "Come on, stand up, they're playing the national anthem."

After the trumpets finish the last note in "home of the brave," the Panthers take the field and whip the ball around the infield. The third baseman tosses the ball to their pitcher, Henderson, a huge kid with bright yellow hair. He fires a few warm-up pitches over the plate, hard and fast. His warm-up pitches look like regular pitches to me.

Josie leads off the top of the first and watches the first pitch go by for a strike. Mr. Shore, who for this game has come out of the dugout, paces the third-base coaching box like a caged tiger. "C'mon, Josie, attack that ball," he yells. Mr. Shore, looking nervous and angry at the same time, pounds his fist into his hand.

Their third baseman adds, "Hey, girl, get that bat off your shoulder." Josie looks at both of them hard and then coolly whacks the next pitch into the hole between short and third for a single. She smiles beautifully from first base. Loretta strikes out on three pitches, but Billy hits one up the middle and Josie scampers to third.

Lloyd is already screaming from the dugout. "We'll cream 'em, we'll cream 'em!" while Mr. Shore continues his pacing back and forth, barking, "Next batter, next batter, get up there." But the rally soon dies as Robert strikes out and Cat taps weakly to second.

In the bottom of the first, Billy appears nervous as he walks the first two batters. Shades of the first game, I think. Mr. Shore must be thinking the same thing as he slaps his forehead in frustration and cries out, "Billy, can't you get the ball over either?"

The third batter tries to bunt the runners over, but pops the ball back to Billy, the runners holding. One down, two on. Billy settles down by striking out the next batter, but our hope to get out of the inning is dashed when the Panthers' cleanup hitter smacks a single through the right side. The ball rolls off Lori's glove, putting men on first and third with one run in.

"Couldn't you hold on to that?" Mr. Shore yells out

122

at Lori, and the poor girl looks crushed, like she did at our very first practice session. Instinctively, I look over to where Mr. Janowicz is sitting and believe I see him sadly shaking his head.

Our infield goes to the mound for a conference. Also our outfield, which I admit is a bit weird. Mr. Shore is already in full stride when I get there. "Is this going to be a repeat performance? Is this what we have practiced for? What are you trying to do to me? I don't want to be humiliated two times in a row—"

"I got an idea," Lloyd says, interrupting Mr. Shore, who gives him an angry look. Lloyd then says to Cat, "Stick near third base. On the second pitch break for the bag and we'll see if I can pick that sucker off."

Mr. Shore starts to say something to Lloyd. I think for a second he's gonna pull Lloyd out of the game for cutting him off. But for some reason Mr. Shore checks himself and just walks back to his coaching box.

On the second pitch Lloyd fires a bullet down to Cat, who tags the surprised runner trying to scramble back. Our whole team cheers, Lloyd loudest of all. The next batter strikes out to retire the side.

We trot back to the dugout. As Lloyd passes by, Mr. Janowicz says, "What a beautiful play, Lloyd. I didn't know you were such a good player." Lynne nods her head in agreement. "It was a nice play, wasn't it?" Lloyd says to everyone in earshot.

When Lori steps up to the plate in the top of the

second, the Panthers' catcher, McDaniels, yells, "Hey, there's nothing but girls on this team!"

Lori, realizing there is no way she can hit Henderson, crouches low trying to draw the walk, but the pitcher's control is too good, and Lori strikes out on three straight pitches.

Lloyd, up next, lifts a short fly to right, which drops in for a single. "Come on, Jeremy, get a hit, you're due," I hear Mr. Shore from the third baseline. (Why does he have to embarrass me in front of everyone, I think as I get ready to bat.) Henderson's first pitch looks inside. I spin away—and touch my eye—but the ball catches the corner for a strike. "What are you afraid of?" I hear Mr. Shore say. "The ball can't bite you."

McDaniels, their catcher, picks up the thread. "Hey, Hendo, we got a chicken up here." Determined, I tap the bat on the plate and then swing wildly at an outside pitch for strike two. The next pitch, again inside, freezes me and I don't swing, but the umpire calls, "Strike three."

"Cluck, cluck," McDaniels says sarcastically.

I walk back to the dugout and don't even dare to look down the line to Mr. Shore. I can feel him staring at me.

"Don't worry, you hit a home run next time," I hear Mr. Janowicz say from near the dugout. Fat chance, I think. Fred, up after me, manages to hit a chopper to short, and Lloyd is easily forced at second for the third out.

In the bottom of the second, Billy finds the range and retires three Panthers in a row, striking out two of the three batters he faces. At least we are not going to be blown out of this game, but we're not exactly scoring runs in bunches either.

In our half of the third, Billy picks up his second hit, this time a double down the line with two out, but is left stranded as Robert grounds out to third.

The play at first is close, so close that I can't tell whether Robert beat the throw or not. While I'm not positive, Mr. Shore is and rushes across the field to confront the umpire who made the call. "What kind of call was that, ump? He had it beat."

The umpire dismisses Mr. Shore by turning his back. This makes Mr. Shore so angry he runs around to the umpire's face and starts to argue again. "Do you hear what I'm saying?" Mr. Shore protests, fairly scream-ing. "He was safe!"

"I hear you," says the umpire. "And if I hear more of you, you'll be out of this game for good."

I steal a quick glance over at the Penwell coach. He is grinning at Mr. Shore's behavior. I can't look again. I feel embarrassed, like the time I once went to my aunt's house for a birthday party and my father put a lampshade on his head. After the umpire's warning, Mr. Shore retreats to the dugout as the Panthers come to bat in the third. He still has some words for the umpire as play continues.

Billy continues to be too strong for the Panthers. Three batters fail to get on, the ball not once getting out of the infield. Josie makes a nice play in the inning, running to her left, grabbing a ball on two hops, and pegging a perfect throw to Robert at first.

In the top of the fourth, Cat opens with a single. Lori strikes out, but Lloyd again singles, with Cat stopping at second. I strike out for the second time, this time on a pitch that is way in the dirt. McDaniels makes chicken noises at me as I walk dejectedly back to the dugout. "Not to worry," I hear Mr. Janowicz call out, but it doesn't help much. Fred ends the inning by hitting an easy comebacker to the mound.

It is clear that the only thing keeping us in the game is Billy, who is pitching magnificently. He has excellent location on his pitches, and there is still a zip to his fastball. Sweat pours down his face as he continues to mow down the Panthers in the fourth, one-two-three.

Yet for all his great pitching, we are still down by one run as we enter the top of the fifth. After Josie and Loretta are easily retired, Billy continues his heroics. He gets hold of a Henderson fastball and rockets it over the fence. "Home run! Home run!" Lloyd screams. Billy calmly trots around the bases like it was nothing. We all mob him at home plate. Mr. Shore raises his fist in triumph, like a general who has captured an important hill. Robert then flies out to end the inning, but at least now the score is tied, 1-1.

The Panthers, now very frustrated, swing at every one of Billy's pitches, but hit nothing but air. The game goes into the sixth and last inning.

"We got 'em now," Mr. Shore says. "Let's move it, now's the time to crunch them," but he wrings his hands in despair as both Lori and Cat ground out.

"Well, I guess it's up to me to hit a home run," Lloyd says as he enters the batter's box. "For Lynne," he adds, waving at her. He then drives the first pitch into the gap between left and center. The ball hits the fence on one bounce and caroms to the left fielder. Lloyd rounds second. Mr. Shore hollers at him to hold it there, but Lloyd, ignoring him, accelerates and slides into third a split second ahead of the relay throw.

"Why did you do that?" Mr. Shore screams at Lloyd when the umpire has called time. "I told you to stop!"

"It's a triple!" Lloyd screams back.

A frightening and startling thing happens then. Mr. Shore goes absolutely crazy then and there. His eyes bulge; his voice becomes even louder, and his hands wave alarmingly close to Lloyd's face. For a second I think he's going to hit Lloyd. The whole stands can hear him as he roars, "Who do you think you are talking to me like that? I told you to stop at second. You disobeyed a direct order. If you can't obey me, get off my field right now. I should have pulled you out before when you interrupted me. But I let it go."

"It's not your field, we're at Penwell," Lloyd points out.

That response totally flips out Mr. Shore. I notice a bright vein standing out in his neck. His fists clench, and he turns a bright red. "I'll take you out of the game right now!" Mr. Shore explodes. "Peggy can run for you."

"Go ahead, see if I care," Lloyd says, practically crying with anger. "I had it beat all the way."

"I'm not interested in your explanations, smart guy. Why don't you just turn in your uni—"

The whole field erupts as the Penwell coach and members of both teams rush into the infield. Just at that moment I see Mr. Janowicz stepping in between Lloyd and Mr. Shore. When did he come onto the field? I didn't see him walk over at all.

"Please, if you will excuse me," he says, tapping his cane. "I do not wish to interfere, but—"

Mr. Shore, startled for a second, steps back and then he says, "Please, Mr. Janowicz, with all due respect, this is none of your business."

Mr. Janowicz turns to face Mr. Shore. "Business, shmissness," he says evenly. "Certainly this is my business. I have an interest in the player what wears my uniform, no?"

"Please, Mr. Janowicz, I am the manager and—"

"You may be the manager," Mr. Janowicz says right

away, "but I do not believe you are aware of what you are doing to the children. Yes, they should respect you, but they must not be afraid of you."

"But—" Mr. Shore tries to say.

"But nothing. You are causing them pain by all this yelling and ordering. All game you do this. I watch you. Is this what a teacher is supposed to do?"

"Get off my field," Mr. Shore orders, completely losing himself. "You are holding up my game."

"No," Mr. Janowicz replies calmly, "it is you what is holding up the game with your ridiculous actions. It is you what is embarrassing yourself. Such nonsense. The young base runner must listen to his manager, but he must also listen to his own judgment too, no? Why are you acting like this? I'm sure you do not mean to hurt the children."

Mr. Shore starts coughing, then trying to answer, his face even more red now.

"Perhaps you would like to calm down for the moment," Mr. Janowicz says sympathetically. "From talking so loud, you cough. Go take a drink water. You will feel better in a minute, I guarantee it."

By this time one of the umpires has come over to see when the game will continue. He takes Mr. Shore and leads him to the water cooler. Mr. Shore is still coughing a lot. The Penwell players trot back to their positions. Mr. Janowicz comes over to me. "Ach, such things to argue about. Lloyd, later you must apologize to Mr. Shore for what you said. You may have shown good baseball thinking, but you were rude."

Mr. Janowicz then puts his hand on my shoulder. "I think Mr. Shore will be all right soon. Now I ask you a question. What do you see when you look at the third baseman?"

"A huge monster," I say.

"No, look with your brain."

"He's playing so far back."

"So?"

I get what he's saying. "A squeeze play?" I say. "You want me to bunt? I can't bunt."

"I want nothing but for you to be happy."

The umpire returns with Mr. Shore, and before there can be any more words between Mr. Shore and Mr. Janowicz, the umpire cries, "Play ball!"

Mr. Shore seems calmer now as he walks quietly to his coaching box. Normal color has returned to his face. He stares straight at Henderson and doesn't look at me or Mr. Janowicz.

As I step in, McDaniels makes even more chicken noises and observes, "What's the matter, Papa Chicken has to come out and help you?"

I ignore his remark and get set in the batter's box. Before Henderson gets ready to throw, I see Mr. Janowicz shortening up on his cane. I know what he means.

I think to myself that I can't show the Panthers I'm

130

bunting because that will draw the third baseman back in and he'll easily throw me out.

I can see Lloyd now dancing off third. "C'mon, Jer, just meet the ball." I know that I don't have a ghost of a chance, but I have to try it anyway. Henderson is going to pitch me inside. I know it, I just know it. I'm afraid of the ball; anyone can see that.

I don't say anything as I let the first two pitches go by for called strikes. "Cluck, cluck," McDaniels says from behind me. From the corner of my eye, I can see the third baseman dropping even farther back. "Look at the ball, Jeremy, look at the ball," I hear Mr. Shore saying, but his tone is softer now, not nasty. I also see Mr. Janowicz nodding his head in approval.

Henderson winds up. I see the ball coming straight for me, way inside, a difficult pitch to bunt. I take one step back, slide my hand along the bat and lay down a bunt that bounces slowly along the third base line. I just stand there. "Run, *tatelah*, run," I hear Mr. Janowicz shout, loud and clear.

I don't know where the ball is, but I run as fast as I can toward first base, expecting at any second to be called out for fouling a bunt on the third strike, or to be called out when the throw beats me to the bag.

When I get to first base, all screaming and jumping break loose. "What happened?" I say.

Lloyd runs up the line, after scoring the go-ahead run, and squeezes me with a giant bear hug. "We did it, we scored! What a helluva bunt, what a squeeze play! What guts, man, on a two-strike count, too." Lloyd keeps shaking my hand until the umpire tells us to resume play.

My ears are ringing with cheers. I see Lynne jumping up and down and Mr. Janowicz waving his cane in the air.

When Fred makes the third out, we realize that only three more outs separate us from victory. As I get my glove to go into center field, Mr. Shore comes over to pat me on the shoulder. "Way to go, Jeremy," he says. "Super bunt. Where'd you learn that? I didn't teach that to you."

"I learned it by myself," I say.

In the bottom of the sixth inning, I can almost hear Lloyd's play-by-play in my head: "OK, sports fans, last of the sixth. Three outs are all that are needed to nail down this win. Oh, oh, the starting pitcher looks like he's tiring, but clearly he does not want to come out of this game. His desire seems to be more than his ability at this point as he has just walked the first two batters, both on 3-1 counts."

Mr. Shore walks purposefully to the mound. I wonder if he's going to start yelling again, but then I see him calmly motioning to Josie at short. Josie trots in and Billy exchanges places with her. "And now pitching for the Card-inals, Number 17, Josie Green-wood," I hear the PA announcement in my mind.

Josie tosses a few warm-up pitches and peers into Lloyd, who sets up a target with his glove. Their third baseman is up first. "Now they got girls pitching—watch it ump, no doctoring the ball with lipstick." Josie answers by whistling three straight strikes by him.

McDaniels, up next, hits a soft fly out to me in center. It's not too difficult a catch, and I pray, "Oh please, don't let me goof this." The ball lands in the webbing of my glove with part of it sticking out, a snow cone. "Cluck, cluck, cluck," I shout happily as I throw the ball back into the infield.

Henderson, the last batter in the game if we get him out, now stands in, and Josie zips one past him for a strike. He grits his teeth and bears down harder. Josie rears back and fires an absolute pill past Henderson for strike two. I feel that Henderson will be looking for that kind of pitch again, but Josie crosses him up by bringing to the plate a very slow change of pace, which completely fools Henderson. He swings so hard, so early for strike three that he practically corkscrews himself into the ground and falls down flat.

Mighty Casey has struck out!

Our team erupts.

Josie is mobbed in one second. Everyone is jumping, yelling, screaming, laughing. Lynne runs over to Lloyd and plants a big kiss on his cheek. Lloyd turns three shades of red, but grins from ear to ear.

"That's it, that's it, we did it," Mr. Shore shouts happily, throwing his cap high into the air. "I couldn't be more proud of you guys—and girls—than I am at this moment. I have won, er—we have won on the field of battle."

The Penwell coach comes over to congratulate Mr. Shore.

"I have to hand it to you, Mark," he says. "You and your team really shaped up. Too bad I gave you a week's postponement after the last game."

"We'd have beaten you even if we played you the next day," Mr. Shore replies with the trace of a smile. "But thanks anyway, Gene. And be sure to tell Headmaster Sorenson how my team outclassed yours."

Then, as if remembering something important, Mr. Shore turns from the Penwell coach and heads for Mr. Janowicz.

"I don't know what to say," Mr. Shore explains to the older man. "I'm truly sorry that I got carried away. You were right. I had no business treating the kids like that."

"No need to be explained," Mr. Janowicz says kindly. Then he changes the subject. "Excuse me, but have you seen my Jeremy? Ah, there you are," he calls out to me. "I want to tell you that I am very happy for you today. Such joy you give me. Such excitement, too. Perhaps more than my doctor would like, too. I go home now to rest."

134

Lynne appears at the shoulder of Mr. Janowicz. "I'll help you, Mr. J. ," she says. To me she says, "You did a great job out there, squirt. Tell mom I won't be too late."

Mr. Janowicz takes my arm for a second. "You come over to the store," he says. "I open soon. We will talk about baseball and the stamps. I have new stamps to show you. You will like them, I guarantee it."

After Mr. Janowicz and Lynne leave to call a taxi, Mr. Shore gets us together for a team meeting. "You guys were great, really super," he says, smiling. "To celebrate I'm treating you all to the best pizza I can find. You guys hungry?"

We all cheer wildly.

The walk to the pizza parlor is one of the best times I've ever had in my life. Loretta tells a new joke: Is baseball worth a lot of money? Answer: Only if it's played on a diamond. We all groan. Then we get delirious with laughter, especially when we all make chicken noises.

"Did you finish your revolutionary war report?" Cat asks me as we walk along. "It's due in seventy-two hours. That's not a lot of time."

"What's to worry?" I tell him.